Painting the White House

Painting the White House

Hal Marcovitz

Copyright 2021 by Hal Marcovitz

All rights reserved. No part of this book may be reproduced or transmitted in any form by any means, electronic or mechanical, including photocopying, recording, or by any information storage and retrieval system, without permission in writing from the copyright owner.

This is a work of fiction. Names, characters, places, and incidents either are the product of the author's imagination or used fictitiously, and any resemblance to any actual persons, living or dead, events, or locales is entirely coincidental.

Printed in the United States of America.

ISBN: 979-8-9855065-4-9

Covered Bridge Press

Contents

1: Inside the Sugar Blush House..9

2: The Buffalo Bill Bedroom..24

3: The Lemon Wedge Oval Room..38

4: The Raspberry Sorbet Room..51

5: The Vanilla Custard Room...64

6: The Chilibean Room...77

7: The Pony Express Room..91

8: The Cirrus Whisper Room..102

9: The Wild Napa Grape Room...113

10: The Kahana Bay Room...126

11: The Vista Mist Bedroom...138

12: The Atomic Winter Office...147

Epilogue: After the Atomic Winter..163

To Gail.

Inside the Sugar Blush House

I first met Janey Robbins about three months ago when she hired me for a painting job. Interiors only. I don't do exteriors, mostly because I hate climbing ladders. Inside, you usually don't need a ladder. You can get away with roller extenders and stilts and step stools. When I need a ladder, like for a stairwell or a foyer, I hire a kid. Kids don't mind climbing ladders. Me? I'm afraid of heights. Did I mention that?

Anyway, Janey didn't actually hire me. Iris Jefferson hired me. Iris Jefferson works for Janey. Iris Jefferson was born in a town in Mississippi named Blue Pickum. She grew up in a shithole cabin with no indoor plumbing. Iris never knew her father. Her mother never hung around Blue Pickum that much, either. Iris was raised by her grandmother. When she was seven years old, Iris was playing in the schoolyard when the school janitor tried to fondle her. The janitor was a creepy guy named Elmo Washington. He was skinny as a maypole, very bald and missing some teeth. Iris told me he was clearly mentally challenged and usually drunk. Iris, who was a big kid even at seven, bit Elmo in the hand and ran home from school. She told Gram Jefferson what happened. Gram Jefferson took Iris by the hand and led her back to school.

"What happened when you got there?" I asked.

"My grandmother found Elmo down in the boiler room of the school. She grabbed a wrench and beat him with it. Elmo was so drunk he never saw it coming. She opened Elmo's head up, right there in the boiler room of the school."

Iris Jefferson smiled when she told me that story. The smile told me that nobody fucks with the Jeffersons of Blue Pickum, Mississippi.

Iris Jefferson was the first member of her family to graduate from high school. She was also the first member of her family to graduate from college. She majored in literature at the University of Mississippi. After graduating from Ole Miss, Iris enrolled in law school at Georgetown University. That's where Janey Robbins found her. Janey went to Georgetown to speak before the African-American Student Union. Iris Jefferson was the vice president of the union and responsible for arranging the event. At the end of her speech, Janey was introduced to Iris by one of the law professors. Janey had an opening on her staff and desperately needed a black face. Her husband, Abe, had been insisting on it for months.

The next day, Janey Robbins called Iris Jefferson and asked her to join the staff of the First Lady.

"You'll love the work," Janey told Iris. "Lots of travel, you'll meet interesting people, eat in good restaurants and you'll never have to wait for a plane."

Iris Jefferson had never been on an airplane in her life. They aren't exactly a common sight in Blue Pickum. To get to Georgetown, she had taken the bus up to Washington from Mississippi. It took sixteen hours and she was carsick the whole way.

Iris had never been in an airport terminal in her life, either. She didn't know airplanes were sometimes late. It had never occurred to her to think about why airplanes might be late.

"But my studies...I really do want my law degree.." Iris started to say.

There was a pause on the line. Iris could tell that Janey had a temper and was trying to suppress it at the moment.

Finally, Janey spoke.

"Honey," she said, "the First Lady doesn't need this shit. If you don't want the job, I'll find somebody else."

Iris decided she could take a year or two off from law school. After all, White House jobs aren't offered to overweight black women from Blue Pickum, Mississippi, every day.

Iris actually enjoyed the work. Janey always took her along when she traveled and made sure she was by her side when the photographers showed up. At first, Iris felt used: she knew she was a token black and

Painting the White House

resented Janey's efforts to showcase her. But Iris soon learned to look past the little indignities. She lost herself in her work and became a much-valued member of the Robbins administration.

Sometimes she wrote speeches for Janey, sometimes she answered her mail. Occasionally, she would lead small tours for V.I.P.'s around the White House. She helped organize Janey's schedule as well as her wardrobe. Janey found out that Iris had a good eye for style and color and when Iris started suggesting certain outfits for certain events, Janey found herself agreeing with Iris's ideas. When the women's magazines started noticing Janey's taste in clothes, Iris Jefferson's opinions around the East Wing started carrying more weight.

By the time I met Iris Jefferson, she was a very powerful figure in the White House. After all, she had just been entrusted with what Janey Robbins told her would be the most important domestic program of her husband's career.

Painting the White House.

* * *

Of course, Iris Jefferson would not be painting the White House. That would be my job. I became a house painter about twenty years ago, right after I got out of college. Did I mention that I have a college degree? I do, in linguistic anthropology. Really, no kidding. Remind me to relate to you my theories about the evolution of language. Anyway, you get out of George Washington University with a degree in linguistic anthropology and what do you do next? Become a linguistic anthropologist? Me? I became a house painter. My first job was with a painting crew headed by a guy named Blackie. We did mostly new construction, which involved spraying watered-down builder's paint onto fresh drywall. First, the builder would tell Blackie how much to water down the paint and then Blackie would water it down even more. I worked for Blackie for maybe a year and learned a lot about the painting business.

Next, I worked for a guy named Whitey. I'm not making this up. You'd be surprised how many guys in the house painting business are named either Blackie or Whitey.

Whitey watered down the paint, too.

In the meantime, I got married. My wife's name was Nancy and she was studying to be a linguistic anthropologist, too. I met her in college. We took a lot of the same courses together and by the time we were seniors we were living together. We had a one-bedroom apartment on the second floor of a converted townhouse on N Street in Georgetown. Nancy had long red hair that reached down to her ass. She was slim and small-breasted and she had really long legs and she liked to wear tight turtleneck sweaters and miniskirts, which were just going out of style at the time. Nancy could really screw. I remember studying for finals and trying to keep my mind on linguistic anthropology and all Nancy wants to do is bang. Maybe that's why I did poorly on my finals that year and couldn't get into graduate school. I was screwing when I was supposed to be studying. Anyway, Nancy was accepted to graduate school. Don't ask me how. She didn't study any more than I did.

So Nancy is in graduate school and I'm working as a house painter and supporting us. One night we come up with the goofy idea that we should get married, so we drove into the Maryland countryside and looked for a justice of the peace who is open. We find a JP somewhere out near Annapolis. He marries us and says he is delighted to do so because out near Annapolis there isn't much marriage work. Most of his time is taken up setting bail for Naval Academy midshipmen who are picked up drunk and disorderly on weekend furloughs.

We are married for about nine months, living in our little apartment on N Street. She studies linguistic anthropology and I am working for Blackie and then Whitey. One day I came home early from a job and walk in on Nancy screwing some guy. I did mention that she likes to screw, didn't I?

I walk in on them just like the guy walks in on his unfaithful wife in the movies. You know, I climb up the steps and hear grunts and gasps, then I open the door and see clothes flung all over the apartment. I see the bedroom door open, and then I see my wife humping some guy. I don't know what to say. I just stand there and stare for a couple of minutes. Then, I say, "Pardon me."

Pardon me?

Well, what would you have said?

The guy climbs down off of Nancy and tells me his name is Franklin Dewey and he is really sorry I caught him screwing my wife. He tells me this as he puts on his pants. He has very thick wire-framed glasses, which he wore during sex. Nancy just sits in bed and smokes a cigarette. She is very sexy, sitting there naked, but I wasn't exactly in the mood for sex at that moment. Franklin tells me he met Nancy at school. He is studying linguistic anthropology as well. Franklin says he totally disagrees with Chandra Srikakulam, who happens to be the guru of linguistic anthropology. He insists to me that the elements of modern language have nothing to do with biological determination, that syntax and phonemes are not genetically transmitted.

"Language is totally determined by environment," Franklin asserts to me while he is zipping up his fly. "I think you'll see some new data coming out soon. There are some people up at Harvard doing marvelous work in the Australian Outback with aboriginal tribes. I think they intend to disprove much of what Srikakulam has been saying."

I want to disagree with him (the balls he has. . . disputing what Dr. Chandra says!), but I wasn't in an argumentative mood. Finally, the jerk leaves the apartment. Nancy asks me what I want to do now. I tell her I want a divorce. She says OK. She hires a cheap lawyer and two months later we're divorced. We split our bank account down the middle and I come out with about $1,600. I take $1,000 and make a down payment on an old Chevy cargo van. I take the other $600 and buy brushes, rollers and drop cloths. Then, I quit Whitey's crew. The first house I paint on my own is out in Chevy Chase. The house is owned by Franklin's parents. Nancy helped me get the job. After that job, Franklin's parents recommend me to some of their friends, and pretty soon I've got a nice little house painting business going on in the Maryland suburbs.

The years pass. My business does well, but I don't want it to grow too big. I want to be a painter, not a painting contractor. I don't want to have to water down paint in order to make a buck. I usually work alone, unless I do a house that has high ceilings. Then, I hire a kid to work up on the ladder.

A few months ago I paint a big old Victorian owned by Hector and Julia Ramirez. Hector Ramirez is originally from Costa Rica and he is very rich. Oil and gas drilling. I think he looks like Desi Arnaz. His wife is from Manchester, New Hampshire. She was born into wealth—I believe her parents own the Red Rooster hotel chain. Anyway, she looks more like Ethel than Lucy. Hector and Julia give a lot of parties and they raise a lot of money for Democrats. Two years ago, they raised $20 million for Abe Robbins. That helped Abe win election as president. To show his appreciation, Abe appointed Hector ambassador to Costa Rica, but

Hector and Julia only spent a year down there. Julia always hated the tropics. When they return from Costa Rica, Julia hires me to paint their house. I do a straight job: I don't water down the paint and I'm really careful not to slop up the terra cotta tiles on the floor of the solarium. Julia and Hector just love the job I do on the old Victorian. Julia tells Janey Robbins that she just had her house painted and she should come over and see it. Janey does. She loves it, too.

A few weeks later, the phone rings and it's Iris Jefferson telling me that the First Lady of the United States wants me to paint the White House.

* * *

Of course, painting the White House is no ordinary job. I know this ten minutes after I hang up the phone after talking with Iris. There's a knock on my apartment door and when I answer, two guys wearing sunglasses and cheap cotton suits are standing there. They are very serious-looking dudes. One guy is tall, one guy is short. They tell me they're with the Secret Service and they had been waiting in a car in front of my building. As soon as Iris finished her conversation with me she called and told them to begin the security clearance. They are here to interview me. I let them in.

They ask me a lot of questions, such as where I was born, where I went to school, what clubs I belong to, what my hobbies are, who my friends are, whether I have any enemies, whether I know anybody who would want to harm the president, that sort of thing. The tall one does all the talking. He tells me his name is Van Buren. He is very friendly.

"You'll like working in the White House," he says.

"I hope so," I answer.

"Really, you will enjoy yourself. How long do you think the job will take?"

"Three months, maybe four."

The short one takes a lot of notes but doesn't do any talking at all other than tell me his name is Webster. I notice he wears a toupee and that he is very sloppy in how he applies it. The hairpiece is a very, very black wig he has plastered on off-center, using too much glue.

Finally, they both rise from their chairs to leave.

"Any questions?" Van Buren asks.

"Just one," I say. "Janey Robbins. . .is she tough to work for?"

Finally, Webster speaks up.

Painting the White House

"She's a bitch," he says. "A fucking black-hearted bitch."

* * *

Janey was born in Philadelphia, the only child of Sam and Sally Goldwick, who are rich because Sam owns a lot of supermarkets. Sam and Sally were wealthy before Janey was born, so Janey never knew poverty or the struggles of poor people. Sam Goldwick was born poor in a rowhouse in West Philadelphia. He dropped out of school when he was fourteen years old and went to work selling fruit for a street vendor. By the time he was seventeen he owned the fruit stand and by the time he was twenty he owned a dozen fruit stands. He was a millionaire before he was thirty. Along the way Sam and Sally Goldwick bought a home on the Main Line. That was the life that Janey was born into, and by her adolescence she was the consummate and complete wealthy American princess.

She was an attractive but not terribly bright young woman whose parents doted on her and made sure life came easy for her. She was born with her father's angular and crude nose, but when she was fifteen Sam paid for a nose job and, suddenly, Janey had a cute little button above her lip. When Janey was sixteen her father gave her a Jaguar for her birthday, and when she was seventeen her father gave her a credit card. When she was eighteen she went away to Penn State, which was the only college that would admit her. Janey's father had tried using his influence to get her into the University of Pennsylvania and then Swarthmore, but when the admissions committees at the two schools saw Janey's grades and her SAT scores, well, not even Sam Goldwick's millions could help her.

Still, Janey enjoyed Penn State: she was, at last, free of her family and off on her own for the first time in her life. She had never been what you would call a rebellious youth, but at home she did bristle under her parents' leash. At Penn State, she learned how to drink beer and smoke marijuana and sleep with men. Janey wasn't very bright, but she was smart enough to keep her grades up because she knew that if she failed, she would have to leave Happy Valley and return home. Sam had warned her that if she flunked out of Penn State, her next stop would be as a checker in a Goldwick's Market. Sam made his checkers wear red and green aprons with their names stitched above the pocket. Janey thought the aprons were hideous.

She often closed her eyes and imagined herself standing behind a cash register, hefting 16-pound turkeys or 24-can cubes of Coke and sliding them across the electric scanner that reads the UPC symbols, feverishly keeping up with the groceries as they were dumped in front of her by one of those black rubber conveyor belts she saw in her father's supermarkets. She hated the smell of those conveyor belts more than anything else. The rubber was porous and it absorbed the odors of the store. Usually, the belts absorbed the fruit and vegetable odors, and it kept those odors long after they were ripe. Janey could always smell rotten apples or putrid grapes on the black conveyor belts at the checkout counters. She couldn't imagine standing next to one of those belts eight hours a day.

Worst of all, though, she had seen her father's checkers at work, and she dreaded how they had to constantly answer the most inane questions, such as whether the peaches or the corn flakes were on sale. Most of the shoppers seemed to be overweight, aging women who called the checkers, "Dear" or, even worse, "Hon."

She could hear it now: "Janey dear, how much are the Oreo cookies? Are they on sale, Hon?"

Of course, they would know her name because it would be stitched across her breast on one of those hideous red and green aprons.

"You can't be serious," Janey said to Sam, when he told her of his threat to make her a checker.

"I'm serious," said Sam.

Janey never took her father's threat lightly.

Janey met Abraham Robbins at Penn State. They took some classes together; Janey noticed Abe mainly because of his good looks, and she also noticed that he noticed her. Finally, Abe approached Janey and asked for a date. Abe was tall and trim and athletic. Janey could tell he was very smart. He wasn't very good in bed, but Janey could look past that.

Abe told Janey that he planned to go to law school and that he wanted to go into politics. His goal was to serve in Congress. Abe's father owned a tiny grocery store in Northeast Philadelphia. The family lived in an apartment over the store. When he was in high school, Abe worked in the store during the afternoons and early evenings. Occasionally, on weekends, he helped out his Uncle Morrie, who was a house painter.

What do you think of that!

Painting the White House

Abe also played quarterback on his high school football team, but he wasn't good enough to win an athletic scholarship. He was going to Penn State on financial aid and student loans.

They were married right after Abe graduated. Janey dropped out of Penn State, came home and spent the last six months of Abe's senior year reading bridal magazines and losing weight. She never did get her degree, but she never had to work as a checker and wear a red and green apron, either.

They had a very elaborate wedding which cost Sam Goldwick a lot of money. There were 450 guests at the wedding, and something like 425 of them were friends of the bride. As wedding gifts, Sam gave the newlyweds a trip to Hawaii and a townhouse in Society Hill. He also paid off Abe's student loans and took care of his tuition at law school. He bought out Abe's father and hired him to run one of his supermarkets. When Abe graduated from law school Sam Goldwick talked to some friends and found Abe a job at a law firm in center city Philadelphia. Two years later, Sam bankrolled his son-in-law's first political campaign and Abe was elected to the House of Representatives.

He was on his way.

* * *

Iris calls three days after the two Secret Service guys had been to see me. She says the security check is finished and Janey wants me to come to the White House. Could I come right over? How do you say no to the First Lady?

So I find a necktie in my closet, and I put it on, and I notice my shoes aren't shined but what am I going to do? I shrug, and then I hop into my truck and drive over to Pennsylvania Avenue, and the guard at the gate tells me to stop. He asks to see some identification, so I show him my driver's license, and while he is looking it over I notice in my mirror that a Secret Service guy with a dog is looking in the bed of the pick-up truck. The dog is sniffing around.

The guard gives me back my license and tells me I'll get a pass soon so that I don't have to go through all this security razzmatazz every day. Then, he points up the driveway and tells me to park right in front of the place, by the North Portico. I follow his directions and park. Iris comes out to meet me. She isn't anything like I pictured on the phone. To be honest, I don't know exactly what I pictured on the phone. Certainly, I never pictured a linebacker in heels. Iris is over six feet tall and weighs at least 250 pounds. She is wearing this very colorful print dress with lots of yellow daisies all over it. It's December, you know, and it doesn't look right for the season. She also wears too much make-up, and she must be using the cologne by the gallon. She smells like peaches. Her earrings are the size of seashells. She wears a lot of rings on two huge hands and her fingernails are painted red in a hard gloss. She takes my right hand to shake it and I see my four fingers, my thumb and three-quarters of my arm disappear inside a ham hock. And she's got a good grip. Painters have strong hands, but I'm worried she's going to break a bone.

"You're right on time," she says.

I smile. Finally, she opens the vise and releases my hand. I quickly give my right hand a glance, just to make sure she gives it all back.

Iris leads me inside. I see Van Buren and Webster sitting in a corridor on Duncan Phyfe chairs. They look bored. I wave and they wave back. A portrait of Betty Ford hangs over where they are sitting. I have no idea where we're walking. Already, I'm lost. You can imagine why. I am soon to learn there are 107 rooms, forty hallways and corridors and nineteen bathrooms in the White House. The building covers more than a million cubic feet. There are four floors. There is a staff of 110 people, not counting the aides who work for the president. Those people number a few dozen. I ask Iris how long it took to learn her way around the White House.

"Oh, my!" she says. "Months and months! They had to give me an escort because I kept getting lost. One time, I was so lost they had to send out a search party." The thought of that little adventure makes her laugh. In fact, she laughs so hard she has to stop walking. She leans over and puts her hands on her knees and then she laughs some more.

This goes on for about a minute. She is laughing so hard she's crying. As she laughs, the rolls of fat all over her body quiver and quake, making the yellow daisies on her dress dance a tarantella. Finally, she quiets down enough to talk again.

"Do you know who found me?"

I shake my head, but I have a feeling I know what's coming.

"The president himself," Iris says, rather triumphantly. "He found me wandering in a hallway. He says, 'Iris, I bet they don't have any houses like this one in Blue Pickum.'"

Painting the White House

Iris arches her back and puts her hands on her hips.

"I says, 'Mr. President, they don't have shit in Blue Pickum.'"

Iris starts laughing again.

We push on.

Ten minutes later I'm sitting down on a Chippendale chair in the Map Room with Janey Robbins, the First Lady of the United States. Iris finds a chair, too, and lets her bulk down easy. Something tells me Iris has broken a few White House chairs.

Janey gets right to the point.

"I want the whole inside of the house done, top to bottom. This place hasn't been painted in something like twenty years and it shows."

She glances toward the ceiling. I follow her eyes. Semi-gloss white, oil-based. I see a lot of cracks along the edges, which tells me the last guy didn't do a good job of scraping off the old stuff.

I give her my best professional nod.

"Julia Ramirez recommended you," Janey says.

I was about to tell her something about the job I did on the Ramirez home, just to make conversation, but I couldn't think of anything to say. Funny how somebody with a background in linguistic anthropology would be at a loss for speech. No matter. Janey wasn't sitting down with me to hear me talk.

"I want some color in the place," she says. "Work with Iris. . .she has a good eye for color."

Janey stands up.

"I've got to meet some Brownies."

She turns to Iris. "Show him around. Maybe he can come up with some ideas, I sure can't."

And then Janey leaves.

I feel awkward. I look at Iris and Iris smiles back at me. It is a comforting, reassuring smile. There is a lot of warmth inside Iris Jefferson. I decide that I like her.

"Come on," Iris says, "we've got a lot of work to do."

She lifts her incredible girth off the Chippendale chair and starts making for the door. I stop her.

"Wait a minute—that's it? How do I know what colors she wants? How much time do I have? When does she want me to start? How do I get paid?"

Iris laughs.

"You and I pick out the colors. You can take as much time as you want but don't make this your life's work. Start tomorrow and I'll see that you get paid."

So Iris and I go over to her office, which is right next to Janey's office on the ground floor of the East Wing. Every First Lady except Hillary Clinton had an office in the East Wing. When Hillary arrived, she decided she wanted to work in the West Wing, which is where the president's staff works. When Janey arrived, the National Parks Service, which maintains the White House, asked Janey where she wanted her office, and Janey told them it didn't matter to her, so they moved her back to the East Wing.

Iris tells me she has worked for Janey for nearly a year and she has never once seen the First Lady in her office. Whenever Janey wants to talk to her, she always comes into Iris' office. Janey has a secretary, though. Her name is Hazel. Iris says Hazel doesn't have much to do.

* * *

Iris and I work through the rest of the day, and then we work through to the end of the week. But by Friday afternoon we have made most of our decisions about the work schedule and about which rooms to do in what order. This takes some thought. After all, Iris tells me, you just can't walk into the Oval Office and tell the president you are there to paint and he has to leave. In fact, Iris advises me to save the Oval Office for last, and to do it on a Sunday.

We decide to pick out the colors right before I do each room.

A word or two about color: on my way over to the White House that first day I stop at a paint store where I have an account and pick up a stack of chips. Anybody who has ever painted their house knows about chips. They are tiny cards that display five or six shades of paint that are very similar. Paint companies make hundreds of shades and they use chips to showcase them. The amount of color on a typical chip is maybe one square inch. From that sample, you are supposed to pick out a color that you are going to paint on maybe 400 or 500 square feet of wall space. Make sense to you? It never did to me, but since I don't own a paint company, I have to live with chips.

And not only that, but anybody who has ever studied a chip knows that they will never find one that says red or green or blue or yellow or

Painting the White House

even violet. Paint companies give very fancy names to their colors. You want red? You won't find it. But you will find Flamingo, Parisienne, Pink Champagne and Foxglove. Blue? No chance, but I personally have used Alaskan Sea, Nanking and Nocturne. Get the idea?

Black is black and white is white? No they aren't, at least not on a chip. On your typical paint chip, black is Obsidian, Charcoal or Espresso. White is Paper Moon, Sugar Blush or Sour Cream. Get it now?

I guess paint companies employ people just to make up the names of their colors. I bet they pay them a lot of money. I think I'd make a good color namer.

One time, while I was out on a job in Silver Spring and applying a coat of Hacienda (sort of a pinkish brown) it occurred to me that Chandra Srikakulam would probably have a big problem with paint chips. After all, here is Dr. Chandra trying to tell people that language is inbred, that we are born with certain biological abilities to speak and develop language, and then the paint companies come up with ways to rename red and blue. Do you think an infant sucking its thumb in the crib stares at the wall in the nursery and says to himself, "My, what a lovely shade of Aqua Foam?" I don't either, and I don't think Srikakulam does as well.

Of course, you don't have to use chips if you don't want to. You can make up your own colors and have the paint store mix them up for you. It's done all the time, but you pay extra for custom colors. Since Janey told Iris not to break the federal budget on this job, we decide to stay with the chips.

So Iris and I sit down with about 500 chips. And before I start each room, we dive into them and make our selections and that is how we pick out the colors for the White House—or, should I say, the Sugar Blush House.

You should understand another basic problem with painting the White House—the place isn't exactly like any other place in the world. It is a museum and an office building and it has living space for the most powerful person in the world. A million tourists a year trample through the State Floor, leaving their scuffs on the baseboards and hand prints on the walls. (I can vouch for that.)

It is also the place where Janey Robbins lives. Iris tells me the best strategy for me to do is stay out of Janey's way. Actually, that won't be too hard. Iris says Janey usually doesn't get up until eleven o'clock in the morning, sometimes noon. I'm usually on the job no later than seven. By noon, my drop cloths are spread, my brushes are dipped and I'm deep into my work.

I also decide to use latex instead of oil paint because latex dries faster and doesn't smell as bad. Iris tells me that Janey has allergies and she might be allergic to fresh paint. She doesn't know for sure, but there is no sense putting Janey in a crappy mood if you don't have to, Iris says. I agree.

Anyway, on Monday morning I show up at the White House to start on the Lincoln Bedroom. The room has a lot of dark walnut Victorian furniture, but most of the upholstery is yellow-and-green Morris velvet. The carpet is dark green and, according to Iris, when Abraham and Mary Todd Lincoln lived in the White House the walls and the ceiling of the Lincoln Bedroom were dark green and gold. (Little-known fact: Lincoln never slept in the Lincoln Bedroom, he used the room as an office although Mrs. Lincoln bought an eight-foot-long rosewood bed with a horsehair mattress for the room.) Anyway, at some point over the years the ceiling picked up a coat of white paint. The trim is white and the walls are off-white. Eggshell would be a good description.

Iris and I decide the ceiling and the walls should be green, but not grass green. We're looking for something in an earthen color with a lot of brown mixed in. We look through our samples. Ivy League is too green, Biscuits-N-Gravy is too brown. We also discard Freedom Trail, Copper Canyon and Wild West Rodeo. Olive Leaf is out and so is Cypress, Wheatley, Gold Ingot, Carmel and Claymont.

But Iris likes Buffalo Bill, which I can best describe as a muted, mustard brown. I go along with her. For the trim, we narrow it down to Rugged Crag, Gristmill and Potting Shed. We can't decide, so we show the chips to Hazel. I lean toward Rugged Crag, Iris likes Gristmill. Hazel, who is delighted to help, sides with me. Iris frowns, but takes her loss good-naturedly. So it is decided. The Lincoln Bedroom will be painted in Buffalo Bill. The baseboard, chair rail, window casings and crown molding will be Rugged Crag.

Iris and I agree it's a good start.

* * *

Monday morning I show up for work. I arrive at the White House early, just a little past seven. It takes me awhile to unload the truck, but I get some help from Van Buren and Webster who happen to be on duty. By eight, I've got my drop cloths, brushes, rollers and everything else at the doorway of the Lincoln Bedroom ready to go. I pick up a gallon of Buffalo Bill in each hand and shove open the door with my rump. Then, I turn around to enter the room.

And I can't believe what I see.

Jodie Robbins, the eighteen-year-old daughter of the President and the First Lady of the United States, is sleeping naked in Mrs. Lincoln's rosewood bed.

I can tell she's naked because she's sleeping on top of the covers.

The Buffalo Bill Bedroom

At first, I don't know what to do. Should I wake her? Should I find Iris and tell her about this? Maybe I should find Van Buren and Webster. Would they know what to do?

While I'm mulling all this over in my mind, I just stand there and stare. After all, she is a babe.

Jodie Robbins has long athletic legs and a tiny waist. Small breasts, but they are firm. They are heaving slowly as she sleeps. Her hair is dark red and kinky and cut just short of her shoulders. I think it is naturally curly; in fact, I know it is naturally curly.

She is sleeping on her side but her knees are drawn up near her chest in almost a fetal position. Her arms are clutching a pillow. The linen was picked to match the room, which means it is an off-white pillow. Cripes, I think, everything in the White House seems to be either white or off-white. You could go snow-blind around this place.

I stare some more at the president's daughter. I wonder whether she sleeps like this all the time. Anyway, I've just about decided to find Iris and tell her about this when Jodie wakes up. Slowly, she lifts herself up on an elbow and stares at me for a minute. She runs her fingers through her tight tawny curls. She exhales, then scowls.

"Who the hell are you?" she asks.

I tell her I'm the painter.

She regards me for a few seconds, then looks down at herself. At this point, of course, she discovers her nakedness. I expect her to scream or grab a sheet and pull it around herself or something like that, but she doesn't react that way. Instead, she folds her elbow back under herself, closes her eyes and clutches the pillow again. She stays this way for about a minute. What can she be thinking? Lord knows.

Suddenly, she sits up cross-legged on Mrs. Lincoln's horsehair mattress and rubs her forehead with her fingers. Her tiny breasts jiggle as she does so.

I am incredibly turned on.

She yawns.

Jodie Robbins points to the floor, across the room. A robe is sitting there in a heap. It is very incandescent: reds and blues and purples and other bright colors framing a collage of white lotus blossoms, all of which is sewn in intricate and painstaking patterns.

The First Daughter shivers.

"Would you mind?" she asks.

I retrieve the robe from the floor and hand it to her. She slips it on quickly and ties a black satin sash around her middle. The front remains open, though, and I can see her breasts. They are framed in black satin that trims the robe.

"I like your robe."

It was the only thing I could think of saying at the moment. I really want to tell her that I like her breasts, but I want to be a gentleman.

She shrugs.

"It's a kimono. The emperor of Japan gave it to me as a gift a year ago. He told me his wife has one just like it. I'm not really supposed to accept gifts from heads of state, but I kept this one."

She sits up on her knees and flattens it out, pushing the wrinkles down toward her hips. She has a very long waist. I find the motion to be highly erotic. I decide the emperor of Japan is no fool; I bet his wife looks bitchin' in it, too.

The kimono has a little pocket. She reaches in and withdraws a pack of cigarettes and a little red butane lighter. She lights a cigarette, takes a long drag and blows the blue smoke out in a gust. I follow the cloud up toward the ceiling and notice the paint around Mary Todd Lincoln's chandelier is cracked and peeling. Instinctively, I reach into my pocket and clutch my scraper.

I know for a fact that there hasn't been any smoking permitted in the

White House since 1993. Somehow, I don't think Jodie wants me to remind her of this.

She takes another drag and then I follow her blue-green eyes to a corner of the room. There is an empty scotch bottle sitting overturned on the green and gold carpet. It has left a tiny stain. Above the stain hangs a copy of the Emancipation Proclamation.

"I guess I should get rid of that," she says. "Lieutenant What's-His-Name was supposed to take it with him when he left last night, but I guess the idiot left it behind."

"Lieutenant What's-His-Name?"

She draws on the cigarette again. The end glows red, then a few specks of gray ash drop onto the off-white bedspread. Jodie notices the mess she has made, but makes no attempt to clean it up.

"I met him last week. He told me his name, but I don't remember it. He's a military attache. . .he works for my father."

She pauses for a few seconds, smiles, and then speaks again.

"He's the one with the real cute ass."

I nod my head.

She laughs girlishly out loud, and then very coquettishly brings one of her red fingernails to her lips. She permits herself a faint smile.

Jodie leans back, closes her eyes, then rolls her head around her shoulders. She extends her arms out in front of her to stretch. The cigarette dangles between her fingers, blue curlicues of smoke drifting toward the ceiling. She yawns again.

"What time is it?"

"Just past seven."

"In the morning?"

I nod.

She scowls again. "Shit," she says.

I conclude that Jodie looks a lot like her mother: same oval face, same eyes, same cheekbones, same nose. I heard Janey had a nose job; I'm sure Jodie had one as well. I close my eyes and try to imagine that I am looking at Janey twenty years ago.

"You won't tell my mother about this, will you?"

I tell her I won't.

"And don't tell Iris, either. Iris is a real dear and I love her, but she has a big mouth. She'll blab."

Painting the White House

I tell her I won't tell Iris, either.

"Thanks," she says.

I really do want to get started on the Lincoln Bedroom, but Jodie appears to be in no hurry to leave. She just sits there smoking, occasionally running her hand through her hair or regarding her fingernails. Finally, I say, "Look, I have to start work."

She nods, but she doesn't leave.

So I start taping the baseboard.

Let me pause here to say that I used to tape the trim and the baseboard completely by hand. It would take all day just to do that—especially in some of the fancier homes I painted. Most of them have real elaborate wainscotting, arched entry-ways, cast iron baseboard grates, tin ceilings, hand-carved window casings and other such features that are known in the trade as painter's nightmare. Finally, I invested in a tape dispenser and let me tell you, I don't know how I ever survived without one. If you ever do some serious house painting, my advice is to use a tape dispenser. Don't be like me.

Anyway, I start using my tape dispenser and Jodie leans forward to watch, resting an elbow on her knee and cradling her chin in her palm. She watches me work for several minutes. I feel awkward. She asks me what I am doing; I tell her I'm taping the woodwork so that when I paint the walls I won't slop up the trim. I have the feeling the whole concept of what I am doing is completely lost on her.

"I have a hell of a headache," she says. "Do you have any Tylenol?"

"No."

She starts playing with her toenails. They are painted in the same hard red gloss as her fingernails.

"My mother doesn't even know I'm in the house. I'm supposed to be at Dartmouth at an interview with the admissions committee. Did you know I was kicked out of Yale?"

I shake my head.

"It hasn't been in the papers," she says as she picks at her red toenails. "Hopefully, it won't be. The people at Yale said they wouldn't make a big deal about it. You know, it would be very embarrassing to my father—to have a daughter kicked out of college. I'm sure his political enemies would have fun with it."

Jodie doesn't look at me while she speaks. She concentrates mainly on her toenails. I have the feeling that getting kicked out of Yale is, to Jodie, no more serious than getting kicked out of the movies for talking too loud. I conclude that Jodie couldn't have cared less whether her failure in academics makes the papers or not. I don't think the political embarrassment her father could face would trouble her that much, either.

I've known Jodie Robbins only for a few minutes, but I can tell that there really isn't that much that embarrasses her.

At the moment, I think what Jodie finds most bothersome is a split cuticle.

"Why were you kicked out?"

Jodie stops playing with her toenails and turns her head so that she faces me. She draws on her cigarette again, stubs it out and lights another. She smiles.

"I didn't keep up my grades. I was there for one fucking semester and I failed every course. Every fucking course! Can you believe that?"

"What was your major?"

"Linguistic anthropology."

I am completely stunned.

"You've got to be kidding!" I blurt out. "That was my major, too! We've got to talk about it sometime. Being a house painter, you know, I haven't had a chance to keep up with the research in the field. What's Dr. Chandra published lately? Do you know?"

She cocks an eyebrow at me.

"Dr. Chandra? Who's he?"

* * *

Jodie has a lot of cigarettes in her kimono pocket. I have a lot of time. She tells me she feels like talking. It doesn't take long for her story to come out.

Her father was already in Congress when she was born. Jodie grew up in a Georgetown townhouse and attended Vermilion Academy, which is the most exclusive private school in Washington. She was spoiled by her parents and grandparents. As a preteen, she went to summer camp in Big Sur. She spent spring break with her mother in Paris. Her friends and classmates were the daughters of senators, ambassadors and Cabinet secretaries. It was hardly what most Americans would consider an average childhood, but Jodie knew no other life. At Vermilion, she was typical of Washington's generation of privilege.

But that all changed when Jodie was sixteen. Her father ran for president that year, and after winning the New Hampshire primary the Secret Service assigned agents to protect the candidate and his family. Jodie was completely unprepared for what happened next. Suddenly, she was accompanied everywhere by at least one Secret Service agent and usually more than one. And they were relentless: they sat in class with her, ate in the school cafeteria with her and even checked out the girls bathroom for her. Jodie often felt foolish at school as she found herself standing outside the girls bathroom door while a fortysomething guy with sunglasses and an Uzi tucked into his belt checked out the potty.

Slowly, she lost her friends. At first, her father's candidacy—and his success in the primaries—drew more people to her and made her much more popular at school. She enjoyed that. Even at Vermilion Academy, the daughter of a presidential candidate was a rarity. But her new-found popularity didn't last long. Certainly, she could still see her friends and share experiences with them, but now she found her times with other young people to be forced, uneasy and anxious. At the age of sixteen, most of Jodie's girlfriends wanted to talk about boys and their dates with them: how far they went, how far they dared to go. For Jodie, boys were completely out of the question. In her junior year at Vermilion Academy, not a single boy asked her out on a date. The same was true for her senior year. She missed her senior prom because she wasn't asked. Right at the age when she should have started dating, when she should have been making her own decisions about clothes, make-up and jewelry, Jodie found herself isolated: there wasn't a single boy at Vermilion interested in dating the daughter of the president of the United States.

Jodie understood.

"Would you dare cop a feel when your chick's bodyguard is in the front seat?" she asks me. "Would you dare put your hand up my skirt when you know the guy in the front seat is armed?"

I can see her point. The fact that neither her father nor her mother were around to help out made it all much worse. At first, they were out campaigning full time. Then, after the election, both of them continued to travel a great deal: Abe, to meet his obligations as the President; Janey, to meet hers as First Lady. As such, they had little time for Jodie and her problems. Except for the Secret Service agents, whom she found to be dull, humorless adults, Jodie was virtually all alone.

Jodie had just turned seventeen when her father took the oath of office. That spring, she graduated from high school. The headmaster at the school asked Jodie to ask her father to be commencement speaker. She did, but Abe couldn't make it. He was going to be out of the country during his daughter's graduation, attending a summit meeting in South America. The White House staff had been touting it to the press for months as the first important test for the president's foreign policy skills. Abe had given an interview to the *New York Times* in which he laid out his agenda for the summit: he intended to be firm with the South American leaders about illegal drugs. He also intended to get tough with them about illegal immigration. The *Times* ran an editorial approving the trip. Abe's popularity in the polls soared.

Problem was, nobody remembered to check whether Jodie needed her father that weekend.

"Sorry, honey, I just can't break it off," he told her. "I'll make it up to you."

He sent the vice president, instead.

Janey went to the commencement, but she had to leave early. She had made a commitment to speak at the annual convention of the American Red Cross, and told daughter it was impossible to cancel.

All the networks covered the commencement. That night, on the evening news, the nation watched as Jodie Robbins accepted her diploma. What the nation had no way of knowing, though, is that Jodie nearly flunked out of Vermilion Academy. Her grades had started falling just before Super Tuesday the year before. By the New Jersey primary, she was on academic probation. That fall, school administrators let her return for her senior year. She was, after all, now the daughter of the Democratic nominee for the presidency. But from early on, it became clear to them that she was having trouble academically. They assigned tutors to Jodie, they dropped her into slow classes and they advised her teachers to go easy on her, but in the end they could not convince her to raise her grades. They tried to approach Janey, but they never got closer to the First Lady than Iris Jefferson.

They told Iris that the First Daughter was not studying; she was not applying herself to her school work. They made it clear to Iris that unless Jodie buckled down, they would kick her out of school.

"I'm sorry to have to bring that ultimatum to you," the dean of women at Vermilion told Iris.

Iris guessed that the Vermilion dean of women was about sixty years old. She was very skinny, with a pancake paste complexion and very white hair, which was parted in the middle and then pulled back into a tight knot behind her head. A vertical crease of pink scalp crossed the top of her head.

The Vermilion dean of women spoke with a southern accent. Iris knew a Mississippi twang whenever she heard one. There was no mistake about it.

Iris disliked her immediately.

The meeting occurred in Iris' East Wing office. She sat quietly as the dean of women went through the story. Occasionally, Iris nodded. Occasionally, she drummed her fingers on the green ink blotter on her desk. Iris was always a good listener.

Finally, the Vermilion people were through with their warnings. Iris smiled, leaned forward and told them, "Cut the bullshit. If you kick Abe Robbins' kid out of Vermilion, every network rug-rat in Washington is going to be looking at your school and looking to see what dirt they can dig up on you."

Iris pointed to the dean. "And let me tell you something else: Iris Jefferson is just the person to make sure they find something."

Iris wasn't sure she could make good on her threat, but she enjoyed bossing people around. She didn't get much of a chance to boss people around in Blue Pickum, Mississippi. Every time Iris threw her weight around she thought of her Gram opening up Elmo Washington's head. Iris liked opening up people's heads. Iris decided that if she had a wrench in her hand at the moment, she would lean across her desk and whack the Vermilion dean of women on the head with it. Iris knew she could open up a very big gash in the bitch's brain.

She laughed at the thought. "Now, I don't care what it takes, but you make sure Jodie Robbins gets her degree come June. Are we clear on that?" Iris uttered her threat in the deepest, blackest Blue Pickum accent she could conjure up. And then she watched the pink crease atop the Vermilion dean's head turn purple.

The Vermilion people said they understood, and Jodie had her degree.

That fall, the First Daughter started college.

***

Iris handled the application process for Jodie, even flying up to New Haven with her for the entrance interview. The Vermilion people had managed to nurse Jodie through her final few months in school, but they could do little to help her transcript look any better than it did. Ordinarily, Yale would not have considered Jodie, given her low grades. But the admissions committee was not about to turn its back on the daughter of the president of the United States. Allowances were made and Jodie was permitted to enroll.

As for Jodie, she was delighted to finally be out of the White House. She felt stifled inside its eggshell walls, unable to be herself—even around her parents. She rarely saw her father, whom she truly did love, and although she saw her mother a bit more often, Jodie and Janey hardly had what anyone would call a healthy mother-daughter relationship. Jodie found Janey bitchy, nosy, condescending and constantly critical of her. Janey thought Jodie was aloof, rebellious and argumentative. Janey recalled her own teen years, and although she remembered them to be anxious and unsteady, she knew she got along with her mother much better than she was getting along with Jodie. Janey genuinely believed that Jodie hated her and she was at a loss as to what to do about it.

Jodie continually looked for ways to avoid her mother. When Janey was home, Jodie stayed by herself, dreaming of a way to escape the confines of the First Family's living quarters on the second floor. When her parents were away, Jodie found the White House cold, empty and without life.

Mostly, she stayed by herself in her room. It was her favorite place in the building. She decorated it herself, picking out the furniture and linens. Her parents let her do that as a high school graduation gift. One of the ushers told Jodie there was a basement full of art work. Jodie insisted on being taken down to the basement to inspect the collection. She picked three pieces to hang in her room and she was very proud of her selection. They were portraits of First Ladies—Abigail Adams, Dolley Madison and Jacqueline Kennedy. Jodie didn't know anything about them—she was hardly a student of history—but she thought they were attractive women and they had style, and she admired them for that.

Still, she found the White House confining. She went for long walks by herself on the South Lawn, but occasionally saw tourists gawking at

Painting the White House

her from behind the black iron fence that surrounds the property, and that would make her run inside. She discovered the solarium on the roof and spent a lot of time by herself up there. She read that there were a lot of secret stairwells and passageways all over the White House. She spent many hours looking for them—poking her head into closets and utility rooms, feeling around the floors and walls for false panels—but, of course, she never found any trap doors.

She found herself going slowly mad in the White House. She was lonely: alienated from the adult world her parents led on the inside and cut off from the young adults in her generation on the outside of the iron fence. She didn't even have the whole run of the house. She was advised by the ushers to stay off the ground floor during weekdays, because that's when the tourists come through.

"They'll want your autograph," she was warned.

Jodie couldn't imagine why anyone would want her autograph.

"I just feel like I'm living in a museum," she tells me. "I'm afraid to sit on the furniture, touch the china or even make a mess in the bathroom. I've tried to make this place my home, but I feel so intimidated by it all."

Jodie longed to be away from her mother and far away from Washington. College, she decided, would be a place where she could mix with people her own age. It would be a place where people could share her problems and be sympathetic. She wanted to learn how to drink beer and smoke cigarettes. She wanted to experiment with marijuana. She wanted to go bra-less and she had an overwhelming curiosity about sex. She desperately wanted to sleep with a guy and she was determined to do so that fall.

Jodie knew, of course, that she would have to out-fox the Secret Service. Still, Jodie was certain that once she settled in on campus and was out of Washington and away from Janey, the agents would ease up. She realized they would never completely leave her alone, but maybe they would let her go to a frat party by herself, or go bar-hopping with friends, or spend the night in somebody else's dorm room.

So when she was accepted to Yale, she demanded that the Secret Service provide her with agents who could pass for college students. The agency complied, sending Jodie two male agents and one female agent, all three of whom were unmarried and youngish-looking. Their names were Steve, Phil and Jan.

Jodie told the three agents she never wanted to see them wearing suits or sunglasses or the little radios that stick out of their ears. She demanded they wear T-shirts and jeans and that they carry books while on campus. She told Steve and Phil to lose the Secret Service haircuts. Jan said she'd let her hair grow out, too.

Jodie also told the three agents she never wanted to see their guns.

"No problem," said Phil. "We can wear ankle holsters; the guns will be tucked in our socks. No one will ever know we have them."

It worked. Once on campus, Steve, Phil and Jan were easily confused for Yale students. Of course, Jodie could never be totally incognito at Yale; she was, after all, the daughter of the president. Occasionally, reporters would follow her around campus and write magazine stories about her. They interviewed her friends. Most of the stories told of a young woman on the go, a young woman reaching adulthood at one of the nation's most hallowed places of learning, a young woman preparing to join her father's world of power and influence. Invariably, the magazine stories were accompanied by photos of Jodie playing tennis on campus, Jodie sitting in a classroom or Jodie joking with fellow students. Jodie hardly ever read the stories; she certainly didn't keep a scrapbook.

As the weeks passed, fewer and fewer reporters showed up on campus. Jodie was grateful for that. She made friends and most of them simply accepted her as just another college kid.

Jodie also found that the Secret Service intended to be even more cooperative than she had hoped. No—Steve, Phil and Jan weren't going to allow her to go a frat party without an escort, but they didn't stop her from going. They simply tagged along, and Jodie found that her three bodyguards were very good at blending into the crowd. They also kept their promises about T-shirts, jeans, haircuts and ankle holsters.

That fall, at Yale, Jodie had more fun than she had known since before the New Hampshire primary. Two nights after arriving in New Haven, she got drunk for the first time in her life. She threw up into a filthy commode in the restroom of an off-campus bar, and although she was so sick that night she could barely stand, Jodie insisted on staying until closing. Jan held her hand while she threw up.

That weekend, Jodie went to her first campus party and that's where she smoked her first joint. Steve looked the other way.

She started smoking cigarettes. Phil warned her that she should be careful about smoking; that she should keep an eye out for photographers. He told Jodie they would love to photograph her with a cigarette dangling from her lips. Jodie never took the advice, and one day the *Yale Daily News* featured a front-page photograph of the First Daughter wearing bluejeans and sitting cross-legged among the fallen autumn leaves on the quad, a book of poetry open on her lap, a cigarette dangling from her lips.

The First Lady called her daughter that night.

"So, now you're smoking?"

Jodie told her mother that it's true, she smokes cigarettes.

"Don't you realize this means that the tobacco lobby will be all over your father's ass now?"

Jodie hung up on her mother.

Meanwhile, Jodie had sex with a half-dozen classmates. She also had sex with her English composition professor, a 36-year-old lesbian. Jodie certainly wasn't the first out-of-control hedonist to hit the Yale campus, but she was probably the first one who had formerly lived on Pennsylvania Avenue in Washington.

Jodie lasted one semester. She never studied and she hardly went to classes. That fall, she failed every course, even English composition.

What could Yale do?

She was home by Christmas break.

The President was angry.

The First Lady was furious.

* * *

"So I've been home these past few weeks," Jodie tells me. "Iris made some calls to see if any schools would take me for their spring terms. Most of the schools she called said they couldn't, that it was too late to enroll—even if I am the president's daughter. But Dartmouth said they'd talk to me, and I'm supposed to be up there right now being interviewed."

"But you didn't go."

Jodie shakes her head.

"I don't want to go. I know what will happen there—the same thing that happened at Yale. I'll just go to have a good time and I'll flunk out of another school. You do that often enough and the press will catch on."

Jodie lights another cigarette, then she speaks again.

"Pretty funny, isn't it? I can't stand it here but I don't want to leave. I'm a pretty sad case, aren't I?"

I don't answer. Jodie blows smoke rings. "Did you know that the son of John Quincy Adams committed suicide? Did you know the children of John Adams, William Henry Harrison and Andrew Johnson died as drunks? I know all that, because when I was very close to getting kicked out of Yale I went to the library and looked up what happened to a lot of the kids of presidents. I think it was the only time I was ever in the Yale library during the entire semester."

She does that head-rolling thing again and then she does that hand-stretching thing again. I have the feeling that she is getting bored with our conversation and that she is thinking about leaving. She speaks again.

"Janey is coming home tomorrow. She'll find out I didn't go for my Dartmouth interview. I guess I'll have to deal with that."

"What are you going to tell her?"

Jodie shrugs.

"I'll probably tell her to go fuck herself."

She smiles at that. And then she slips out of bed, retrieves her empty scotch bottle and leaves the room.

* * *

It takes me the rest of the week, but I do finish painting the Lincoln Bedroom on schedule. I use four gallons of Buffalo Bill, and I must say that it was an excellent choice. It really brings that room to life. When I finish, I call Iris in and show her. She is delighted. Later that day, Janey comes in to inspect. She says she likes it, too. She promises to bring the president around to see the room.

I don't see Jodie again that week. I ask Van Buren and Webster how she is doing, but they say they don't know. I'm sure they know, but I think Secret Service agents follow some kind of code to keep secrets about the First Family to themselves. After all, how many tell-all books have been written by ex-Secret Service agents? None come immediately to my mind. The Secret Service, I conclude, is very secretive.

Anyway, I keep my eyes and ears open around the White House all that week, but I never hear from Jodie again. I hope she's doing OK, whether it is here or at Dartmouth or wherever.

I also hope she holds on to that kimono. She sure does look great in it.

Painting the White House

* * *

My next job is going to be the Yellow Oval Room. It's a room the president uses for little parties, mainly to receive dignitaries. It's supposed to be used for formal affairs, but I find it to be cozy and intimate. The Louis XVI furniture really looks great in there. So does the Italian marble mantel. If I am ever elected president, I intend to buy a box of good cigars and sit in the Yellow Oval Room and smoke. I will repeal the White House rule against smoking and negotiate a peace treaty with the Cubans so that I may enjoy a fine cigar in this magnificent room.

Iris and I both agree the shade of yellow the last painter used is not bright enough. It has given the room a dull, lackluster appearance, even though three floor-to-ceiling windows provide the room with plenty of natural light and a breathtaking view of the Washington Monument. I make a mental note to work late at least once so I can see the monument from this room at night. Anyway, Iris suggests something a bit more gay, a bit more saucy. I'm with her a hundred percent on this. So we dive into our chips and after much deliberation, we narrow it down to Midas Touch, Neon Light, Citron Glaze and Lemon Wedge. I vote for Midas Touch, Iris insists on Lemon Wedge. This time, Hazel sides with Iris, and Lemon Wedge is the choice. We decide to stay with an off-white for the trim. Iris leaves that choice up to me. I pick Cocoa Shell, which I believe would look terrific on the oval ceiling medallion in the center of the room. An elaborate bronze and crystal chandelier dangles on a swag below the medallion. I'm told it dates back to 1820. You have to see the chandelier all lit up; it is very impressive.

But wouldn't you know it? First thing Monday morning, as I arrive for work, I find the president's chief of staff dangling from that very elaborate bronze and crystal chandelier, attempting to kill himself.

The Lemon Wedge Oval Room

Cripes!

The guy has looped one end of his belt around an arm of the chandelier and tied the other end around his neck. He had been standing on one of the Louis XVI chairs and I guess he just kicked it over. The chandelier is heavy and held onto the central medallion by big lag bolts and, I guess, Number 12 Romex, so it is clear the chandelier isn't coming down from the ceiling. He is still alive, struggling. He is desperately pulling at the leather belt around his neck, trying to free himself. I guess he has second thoughts about going through with his suicide.

The Yellow Oval Room has a high ceiling, which means I need a ladder to paint the central medallion. Reluctantly, I brought a ladder with me today. Did I tell you how much I hate getting up on ladders? I mentioned this to Iris the other day and told her I was thinking about hiring a kid to do the work up on the ladder, but she said that would be a bad idea because it means the Secret Service would have to interview the kid and do a background check and all that would take three or four days. In the meantime, the job is shut down. So what can I do? It's me who has to go up the ladder, nosebleeds notwithstanding.

I have a stepladder standing against the wall in the corridor. I move fast. I dash out to the corridor, pick up the ladder and in an instant I'm back in the Yellow Oval Room and I have it set up. I scamper up the steps in seconds and grab the guy around the waist and hoist him up a bit, enough to relieve the pressure around his neck. He is all blue. With my other hand, I reach into the pocket of my overalls and find my painter's utility knife, which has a new blade. I just changed it that morning before loading the truck for the trip over to the White House. He's lucky I did that, because the new blade slashes right through the leather belt on the first swipe. He's also lucky that Van Buren and Webster let me bring it into the White House. It's in my pocket as I'm walking through the metal detector and the thing starts ringing like a goddamned high school cafeteria bell. Van Buren makes me empty my pockets and when he finds the knife he nearly shits a purple rock. I tell him I've got to have the knife, that no painter can be without his utility knife. Finally, Van Buren relents and lets me into the White House with it. Webster says if I try something funny with my painter's utility knife he'll make sure I eat the blade. He makes me shudder. Anyway, it is lucky for me they let me bring it into the White House, and lucky for the guy I just found hanging from a chandelier.

I cut the belt and the guy collapses onto my knee. Good thing he's a skinny little runt; my guess is he weighs less than 140 pounds.

I ease him to the floor and then go back to work on the belt with my knife, cutting it away from his neck. He starts coughing, gasping for breath. "Let me find some help," I tell him.

I get up to leave, but he waves his hand and says, through his coughs and gasps, "Don't go...don't go." Then, he tries to stand up, but collapses to his hands and knees. I help him onto one of the Louis XVI chairs. I'm worried that he'll throw up all over it. If he does, I intend to tell Iris it wasn't my fault and that she better fix it with Janey.

I notice he has an ugly red welt around his neck. It must be painful.

"Really," I say to him, "you must see a doctor. I'm sure there is one in the building somewhere. I'll find Iris, she'll know what to do."

By now, he has stopped coughing, although he is still short of breath. He is perspiring and his complexion has gone from blue to ashen, although I can tell his color is returning, albeit slowly. He has dribbled down the front of his white shirt and ruined his tie, which is very expensive silk, dyed red and blue. His suit jacket is torn around the sleeve. Is it possible I did that when I slashed the belt? His salt-and-pepper gray-brown hair is disheveled. In short, he's an awful mess.

"Please don't leave," he says. "I just tried to kill myself. I would prefer that people around here not know about that. OK?"

"Well, OK, I guess," I answer.

The Yellow Oval Room has a liquor cabinet. I poke around in it and, sure enough, find a bottle of club soda. It is warm, there is no ice, but I'm sure he'll enjoy it. I pour a glass.

"This may help," I say.

He takes a long drink, drains the glass and asks for more. I fill up another glass and he drains that one as well. He says the carbonation feels good on his throat, which is very sore at the moment. I can imagine. Finally, he finishes drinking. He is even able to smile, sort of.

"Thanks," he says. "That did help. And thanks for saving my life."

I nod. He rubs the back of his neck. I bet that hurts, too. He is, after all, no youngster. I put him at about forty-eight, maybe fifty or fifty-five. Somewhere in there. Who knows how long he was hanging there? Maybe the fact that he is such a little guy and doesn't weigh much is what really saved his life.

"You will keep what happened here a secret, won't you? The president shouldn't know about this. OK?"

"Well, OK, I guess," I say.

He rubs his face. I hope he is planning to leave soon, because I really have to begin work. I feel sorry for him, but I don't have the time to chat. Maybe if he had Jodie's body and he was wearing a kimono given to him by the Emperor of Japan and his boobs are hanging out, yes, I could find time to talk. But he doesn't look anything like Jodie.

Still, he sits there.

"Do you know who I am?" he asks.

He is, of course, Warren Adams, the president's chief of staff. I know this because I've seen him on the evening news. He is a former congressman and a long-time friend of Abe Robbins. They were freshmen in the House together and they served side by side for a dozen years. They grew in stature together over the years and they each became political forces in Washington. When Abe was elected to the Senate, Warren stayed behind in the House, but he moved up to an important committee chairmanship. When Abe was elected president, Warren resigned his seat and went to work for Abe as chief of staff.

He was quickly recognized as the man with Abe's ear: He became the president's confidant, his friend, his adviser, his ally. Warren Adams has an enormous amount of influence on Capitol Hill and Abe relies on him to round up votes. Right after Abe was elected, during the transition, they planned the administration together. Abe never makes an important decision in his presidency without first checking with Warren. At Washington cocktail parties, it is often whispered that Warren Adams is the co-president and—at the more exclusive parties—it is sometimes whispered that Warren Adams is the real power in the Oval Office. For his part, Warren does not dissuade that type of talk. After all, he has ambitions of his own.

Of course, that is not the Warren Adams I am sitting across from at this moment. This most powerful of Washington insiders, this confidant of the president, this king of Congress, is hunched over in an overstuffed antique chair, gargling club soda and sweating under the armpits because the guy who was hired to paint the White House has just caught him trying to do a fandango with the devil.

"Did you know that when I got up this morning, I decided to kill myself? I almost did it at home, but I didn't want my wife to find my body."

"So you decided to do it here?"

He nods. "I checked the White House appointment schedule when I arrived this morning; I knew there was nothing scheduled for this room—no visits by dignitaries, heads of state, that sort of thing. I thought I could kill myself here and nobody would find me for a week. Somehow, that plan all made sense to me this morning. I guess it sounds very silly now."

It sure does. The reason the usher's office kept the Yellow Oval Room clear today is because I told them I'd be painting here. Of course, Warren had no way of knowing that.

"Why did you use your belt?" I ask. "If I hadn't come along when I did, you probably would have dangled there for another hour before you died. It seems to me that would have been a painful and horrible way to die."

He shrugs his shoulders. "I thought about using a gun, but I knew I'd never get it past the metal detector at the front door."

* * *

"Warren? I didn't expect to find you here!"

It is Iris. She is standing at the door. "I came in to make sure our favorite painter was getting off to a good start. Is everything OK?"

Warren Adams nods.

"Everything is fine, Iris. I was just walking by the room when I saw him working. I came in for a peak and we started talking. This fellow is one smart guy—he knows about a lot more than just paint."

He smiles at me.

Iris doesn't appear as though she is buying it. She hasn't taken her eyes off the president's chief of staff since she entered the room. She knows something is wrong.

"You don't look well, Warren," she says. "How do you feel?"

"I woke up with some stomach cramps, but I feel fine now. Really, Iris, I'm OK. I was just leaving; I don't want to keep this fellow from his work too much longer."

"You know best, Warren," she says, and then she leaves.

He turns back to me. "I do feel fine now and I know you have a lot of work to do. Maybe I should go."

He says it, but he doesn't mean it. I soon learn that while Warren Adams may have been feeling better, he had no intentions of letting me get back to work. He was a man who had just tried to kill himself. He was, in fact, a very powerful man who had just tried to kill himself in the place where the president of the United States lives. People of Warren's ilk don't decide to do things like that unless they have a very good reason or, at least, what may seem like a very good reason to them.

I can tell he wants to talk about it. I glance down at the can of Lemon Wedge I brought into the room with me that morning. It will have to wait. Warren Adams needs a good listener. I guess I'm a good listener. As I am learning very quickly, there aren't many good listeners in the White House.

* * *

"Abe is forty-eight, you know," Warren tells me. "I'm fifty. Abe isn't having an easy time of it in the polls. The public is angry. Ha! Isn't the public always angry? They are hungry for change. Still, I think he'll squeak another four years out of this job. In fact, I'm pretty confident about it. The Republicans are in a sorry state right now; they have no national leadership, no agenda, no idea where their party is headed, no idea how to unite themselves at their next convention. It would take a miracle for them to beat Abe next year. Frankly, I don't think there are many miracles out there for them."

I was glad to hear his assessment of the political picture in America. I have grown fond of the people in the Robbins administration in the few short weeks I had been working in the White House. I don't know much about politics or government, but at this point I am fully supportive of the Robbins presidency.

Warren continues.

"I see Abe serving until he's fifty-three. I'll serve right along with him. I'm loyal to Abe, you know. I'll stick this out with him."

He stands up and walks over to the floor-to-ceiling windows. The room is, by now, bathed in the morning sunlight. He stands at the windows, staring at the Washington Monument, which is on the horizon over the railing of the Truman Balcony. The yellow sunlight pours in around his slight frame, which forms a thin silhouette amid the harsh solar glare entering the room.

"I'll be fifty-five at the end of Abe's second term."

"What will happen then?"

"I guess we'll be stuck with the Republicans for eight years," he says. "Politics is cyclical. First we get in, then they get in, then we come back, then they come back. It's been that way for as long as they have been against us and we have been against them. It's going to stay that way for a very long time.

"The public may give Abe another four years, but it won't accept his party and its ideas after that. The public will never tolerate another four or eight years of a Democratic administration once Abe leaves office. The voters will insist on having change by then. The Republicans will appeal to them and they'll promise everything Abe couldn't or wouldn't deliver, and the public will buy their bullshit, and so will the media, and five years from now when Abe leaves office we'll have a Republican in the White House."

He turns away from the window and faces me again. He rubs his neck; it must still be very sore.

"Do you know what will happen next?"

I shake my head.

"Another eight years will go by and then the public will be clamoring for change again. Then, we'll make the promises and we'll sell the public our bullshit. Of course, we'll pull out all the stops so that we make sure we don't blow an election—we have done that in the past, you know."

He cradles his right elbow in his left palm and rubs his chin.

"We'll have to give them something on Election Day the Republicans couldn't possibly give them."

"What will that be?"

He smiles.

"Right now I can't tell you, but I can guess. My guess is, next time, it will be a very, very young candidate: Somebody in their 30s. Or maybe early 40s. The public isn't going to keep buying candidates in their 50s, 60s or 70s. Mark it down. You heard it from me first—eleven years from now, the Democratic Party of the United States will nominate a very young candidate for president. The youngest ever. It is an interesting thought. Don't you agree?"

I shrug my shoulders. To be honest, I hadn't given it that much thought. Painters don't often involve themselves in political theorizing. We are, in fact, a very apolitical lot. We don't even have a lobbying organization in Washington. I am about to tell him this when he cuts me off.

"I'll be sixty-three years old then. And after our very young president serves out an eight-year term, I'll be seventy-one. Then, the Republicans will win the White House back for another eight years after that. Remember, politics is cyclical. By the time we win the place back again, I'll be seventy-nine—probably forty years older than what the party will be looking for in its next candidate."

By now, I could see his point. He had simply missed his opportunity. One candidate from his generation was destined for the White House, and Abe Robbins won the prize. Not Warren Adams.

"You'll be too old to run for president," I said.

He lets a very tiny smile curl across his lips. It is almost a smirk.

"Do you want to know something else? I was twice the congressman that Abe Robbins was. That's right. I was much better at writing legislation, understanding legislation and convincing people to support the legislation that I wanted them to support. Up on the Hill, everybody always considered Abe Robbins to be a lightweight when it came to that part of the job.

"When he went to the Senate, I took over the Ways and Means Committee. The Ways and Means Committee! And I was the chairman! Abe never served on an important committee in his life; he never joined the leadership in Congress. If he had stayed on in the House, he would never have accomplished what I accomplished there."

He rubs his neck again. I wasn't sure what he found more painful: the brush burn from his belt or the thought of losing out in the great game of life to Abraham Robbins.

"Do you know why he's president and I'm not?"

I tell him I don't have a clue.

"He looks better on TV than I do. He's a tall, good-looking guy with a pretty wife and a rich father-in-law who was able to bankroll his elections. He mixes well with rich people and he tells poor people what they want to hear. I can do that, too, but they like the sound of it better when it comes from him. I'm a short, skinny, ugly man. The public doesn't want to vote for ugly men. Didn't you know that?"

He wanders over to the French doors that open onto the Truman Balcony. He stands there for a moment, staring out at the South Lawn. I walk up behind him. Over his shoulder, I can see President Robbins. He is dressed in a blue and white sweatsuit, and he is jogging on the running track that Bill Clinton had installed around the South Lawn. Across the president's chest are the words "Penn State." Behind him, three Secret Service men try to keep up. One of them is Webster. He is having the most trouble keeping pace with the president.

Warren ponders that scene for a few minutes. Finally, he says, "I'll never be president."

The way he puts it, well, it makes perfect sense to me. I feel sorry for him. After all, I failed early in life—I was twenty-one years old when I found out that I would never be a linguistic anthropologist. It was tough to take, for sure, but I was young enough to get on with my life. Now, I have an honest business, I make a comfortable living, I'm my own boss and right at this moment I'm working on the painting contract of a lifetime.

Warren Adams found out late in life that his destiny was to fail. Sure, he had been a powerful guy in Congress, he'd been chairman of Ways and Means, he was all that and more. But what he really wanted was to be president and he realized at the age of fifty-one that he would never make it. He was a failure: he knew it and the only thing he could think of doing about it was to kill himself. He has my pity.

Still, I've also heard enough of his whining. "Is that any reason to kill yourself?" I ask. "Lots of people run for president. How many of them commit suicide when they don't make it?"

"Probably very few," he says. "Maybe I would have been the first. Hey! That would have gotten me into the history books. What do you think about that?"

* * *

He asks me if he could have another club soda. I find the bottle and pour him a glass. He finds a seat on a Louis XVI chair. He looks weary, which I can understand. He has been through a lot this morning—he has come to terms with his own future and hasn't liked what he has seen. That would be enough of a day for most people, but this guy tried to top it all off by killing himself. Before he leaves, I think I'll tell him he should take the rest of the day off. I think he needs it.

As I am handing him the glass of club soda, a voice at the doorway says, "Warren? Are you OK? Iris called a few minutes ago and said you looked as though you were ill. How are you feeling?"

We both turn to face our visitor. A tall man in a charcoal gray suit is standing at the door. I'd say he is forty years old. He is developing a paunch. He is going bald very quickly. He wears very thick eyeglasses.

"I'm fine, Franklin," says Warren. "Really, I was just heading back to my office."

He rises to leave, smiles at me and extends his hand. We shake.

"Thanks again," he says.

Both men leave.

I had, of course, recognized Franklin immediately. It was the same Franklin I caught humping Nancy nearly twenty years ago. He is older now and fatter and balder, but there is no question it is my old friend Franklin. As I spread my dropcloths around the Yellow Oval Room and tape the woodwork, I find myself delighted to have seen him again; it has made me feel young and full of zest. When I get to be Franklin's age, I tell myself, I hope I don't look like him. The joke here is that I am already Franklin's age and I don't look like him. This gives me a good feeling.

I also expect Franklin to return to the Yellow Oval Room as soon as he realizes who I am.

It takes ten minutes.

I assume he walked Warren back to his office and then immediately returned to the Yellow Oval Room.

"I never thought I'd see you again," he says.

Painting the White House

"Well, I never thought I'd meet up again with the man who ruined my marriage."

"I'm still sorry about that," he says. "No hard feelings?"

"None from me. I got over Nancy long ago."

"I'm glad to hear that."

I open a can of Lemon Wedge and start stirring. I have a dozen cans of Lemon Wedge with me today: it will take that much paint to do the Yellow Oval Room. As such, I can't box the paint today. Boxing the paint is when you take every gallon of paint and mix them together all at once and then you work from one large container. It blends all the gallons together so that you can work with one even shade. You'd be surprised how much one gallon can be off in tint from the next gallon. You may buy twelve gallons of Lemon Wedge from the same paint store, but you should know that you are going to come out of the store with twelve variations of Lemon Wedge. The guy who mixes the paint at the store just can't mix every gallon evenly—it is humanly impossible. You can't tell it by looking at the paint in the can, but once you have it on the wall you will be able to see the difference. This problem is a lot more common than you would think. The solution is to box the paint, but that works if you have only two or three gallons for the room. When you have a dozen gallons, like I do today, you can never find a container big enough to hold twelve gallons, so you have to work from gallon to gallon. I'll use the first gallon until I have about a quart remaining, then I'll pour paint from the second gallon into the first and work with that until I have about a quart remaining. Then, I'll pour the third into the second, the fourth into the third, and so on. It's tedious, but when you have a room this size you have to do it this way.

"So what are you doing here?" I ask Franklin. "Do you work here now?"

He nods his head. "I've been working for Warren for nearly twenty years. I took a job on his staff right after he was elected to Congress. I stayed with him all those years, and when he left to come to the White House I came with him. I'm his chief deputy."

There is a certain glimmer of pride in the way he says it. I can tell he is extremely proud of his work and delighted with the fact that he has a reserved space in the White House parking lot. Good for him.

"So you work for Warren Adams? Funny, but I remember that you were studying linguistic anthropology. What happened? Why didn't you stay with it?"

Franklin shrugs.

"After graduate school I couldn't find a job. I applied for a number of university teaching positions; it seemed to me that I was qualified for the jobs and always interviewed well, but I was invariably turned down after the head of the linguistics department read my thesis. I couldn't understand why I kept losing out on those jobs, but after awhile it hit me: it was my thesis. Nobody in any university linguistics department had any interest in hiring somebody who disagreed with Dr. Chandra. I was twenty-three years old and already washed up in linguistic anthropology. Can you believe that?

"So my dad talked to some people he knew and found a job for me as a congressional aide on Warren's staff. I've been with him ever since."

He tells me that he enjoys his job and respects Warren, and that it is his feeling Warren will run for president soon. He is looking forward to that because he believes Warren would make a terrific president. Franklin predicts that Abe will serve another term and that Warren will then be elected president of the United States. Franklin is looking forward to a big job in the administration of President Warren Adams.

We talk that over for a few minutes and then I start dabbing my roller into a tray of Lemon Wedge, which I hope Franklin will take as a message that I want him to leave. He picks up on the hint and starts walking out the door.

"One more thing," I call after him. "Ever hear from Nancy again?"

"Absolutely," Franklin says. "We're married."

That sort of stuns me, although I am at a loss to explain why.

"How is she?"

"She's fine, just fine. She teaches linguistic anthropology at George Washington and she is on track to head the department. She's written two books on linguistic anthropology; they both sold well, even though they were academic books. Her publisher is very happy with her and wants her to write another book. She's doing the research right now."

"Were they good books?"

His expression turns sour.

"No," he says. "I read them both. As far as I can tell, she broke no new ground in either book. She agrees totally with everything Dr. Chandra says. I guess the world of linguistic anthropology is not ready for a maverick."

"Guess not," I say.

He turns to leave, but stops at the doorway.

"I can't say I'm very happy with her."

"Really? Why not?"

"I'm certain she fucks other guys."

* * *

Despite my late start on that first day, I manage to finish the Yellow Oval Room on time. Iris came around to see it while I was working and asked me what I talked about that first morning with Warren Adams. She says there are a lot of rumors floating around the White House about what Warren was up to in here. He had gone home sick that day, she says, and didn't return until late in the week. When he came back to work, his head was clamped in a neck brace. Warren has told everyone that he woke up with a very stiff neck one morning and that his doctor is making him wear the brace.

Iris tells me there is a lot of skepticism in the White House about that story. She says that some of the reporters down in the pressroom had even brought it up during the daily media briefing.

"So what did you two talk about that morning?"

"Nothing special. He said his wife wants their house painted and he was asking me questions about it. He may hire me; we were going over prices. It was all pretty routine."

Janey comes by late in the week and looks the room over as well. She says she loves it. She also tells me that she had shown the Lincoln Bedroom to the president and he is impressed with my work as well.

"Eventually, I'm going to get to his office," I tell her. What color do you think he'd like?"

Janey says it doesn't matter with Abe, any color would do.

"That sort of thing isn't important to him," she says.

I find that a bit odd, but I keep my opinion to myself. Around the White House, I have learned that is a wise strategy.

* * *

Franklin stops by the Yellow Oval Room a few times as well. He says that he told Nancy he ran into me in the White House and that she was delighted to hear I'm well. Franklin says Nancy suggested that it was time they had their apartment painted again, and there is no reason I shouldn't do the job. After all, she has always believed I had talent as a house painter. Nancy wants me to come over to their apartment during the day with some samples, Franklin says.

"She said to tell you that she has plenty of time between classes to meet with you, so that's no problem."

"Do you want to see the samples, too?" I ask.

"I'd like to, but I can't get away from the White House long enough. I'm sure you and Nancy can handle things without me."

I tell him that I am sure we can.

* * *

"It looks like a fire engine," Iris says.

I agree. The Red Room is painted in the reddest red I have ever seen. It is a very elegant room, with richly carved wood fronts on the early 19th Century Gothic furniture. First Families often use the Red Room as a sitting room or for small dinner parties. I am most impressed by the hardware on the furniture—you know, catches and pulls. It is all very decorative brass, forming dolphins, leaves, lions' heads, sphinxes, that sort of thing. There is also a very grand fireplace in the room, a 36-light chandelier hanging overhead and a portrait of Dolley Madison looking over the whole room. And, of course, all that red.

Iris and I decide the Red Room has to be a red room, but it doesn't have to be such a very red room. Our first choice is Rugosa, but that has too much orange in it. Rose Chintz has less orange, but borders on brown. Pink Hibiscus comes close to what we are looking for. Ruby Gem is too red. Royal Plume is too purple. Finally, we decide on Raspberry Sorbet. It is a muted, mild red. Not too orange, not too brown, not too purple and, best of all, not too red.

We don't even have to go to Hazel on this one. For the woodwork, which is quite elaborate in the Red Room, we decide to be bold: we chose a very deep gray. We think Stonecutter works the best.

"I think Janey will really like our choice," says Iris. "When I told her we were planning the Red Room, she told me to be careful on that one because the Red Room is one of her favorite rooms and red had always been one of her favorite colors."

Well, Iris is wrong about that.

Black is definitely Janey's favorite color.

The Raspberry Sorbet Room

I don't often oversleep, but on the day I'm supposed to start on the Red Room the damn clock doesn't go off. So I'm already an hour late by the time I roll out of bed. Cripes, I hate being late.

What happens next? Wouldn't you know it but the damn truck won't start? It's January and cold out this morning, of course, which I'm sure has a lot to do with why it won't start. Cripes. Anyway, what should I do now? If I call my repair guy, I'm going to be really late. I take my phone out of my pocket and start punching in the number for my repair guy, but then I hang up before the first ring because I have a good idea. I own a motorcycle and keep it in a garage around the corner from my apartment building. All my tools and paints are already at the White House, so I really don't need the truck. Why don't I give myself a treat today and ride my bike in?

I'll need a warm jacket because it's cold out this morning. I have a black leather biker jacket with a down lining. I also have a pair of leather biker gloves that are very warm as well. I find my biker boots and now I'm all set. I grab my helmet and I'm on my way.

The bike starts right up. It's a black and chrome Triumph TR6, which is a vintage model I picked up used about five years ago. Call me middle-age crazy, but ever since I was a kid I wanted a motorcycle. One morning, I wake up and decide it's time I ought to have one. I spent many weekends restoring the bike, chopping it and fitting it with some truly righteous gear. It has a funky 500 cc engine, a twin carb head and dual mono-block carbs, pop-up pistons, big valves, a trick cam and glass-lined pipes. I have a Cheetah sissybar and a king-and-queen saddle, a shorty front steel fender and a pair of nasty spool mag wheels. Let me tell you, it's one beastly machine. I use it as a touring bike and a sporting machine. I take it out mostly on weekends for long rides in the Maryland and Virginia countrysides.

Of course, today I am negotiating the streets in the District of Columbia. It's not the type of bike riding I prefer, but I still enjoy the trip into work. Finally, I pull into the gate off Pennsylvania Avenue and the guard signals me to stop. Suddenly, I'm surrounded by White House police and Secret Service agents. The Secret Service guys actually have their hands in their coats and I know they are fingering their Uzis. Cripes, I think.

Out of the crowd steps Van Buren and Webster.

"Off the bike, mister," says Webster. I notice that today he has been particularly sloppy with his toupee. I mean, he has plastered it on too far forward. The wig seems to cover much of his forehead, hanging down right over his eyes. Doesn't he use a mirror when he puts the thing on every morning?

I always suspected Webster has a mean streak and that he secretly hopes somebody will take a shot at the president simply because it will give him an excuse to shoot back.

I raise my hands slowly off the handlebars. I take off my helmet and at that point everybody sees it's me, the painter. Much relaxation all around, except I detect a sincere look of disappointment in Webster's eyes—or at least in as much of Webster's eyes as I can see.

Van Buren laughs and motions for everybody to go back to their posts. "Don't be a wiseass," he tells me. I shrug my shoulders, kick the engine back on and motor up the driveway. I decide it's best to be discreet, so I drive around back and park the bike by the South Portico, right under the Truman Balcony.

Ten minutes later I'm in the Red Room stirring up a gallon of Raspberry Sorbet. What with sleeping in and having the truck trouble and getting stopped at the gate, I'm off to a late start so I plan to work hard today to catch up. It's already after eleven o'clock. I decide to work through lunch to make up for lost time. No big deal about that. After all, I have left my lunch in the truck, anyway.

Painting the White House

So I'm hunched over a can of Raspberry Sorbet and I'm stirring it up and I get the feeling somebody is watching me. I turn around and see Janey Robbins standing in the doorway.

The First Lady is sort of leaning against the side of the doorjamb, her arms crossed across her breasts, her hands resting on her shoulders, and she smiles when she sees I have noticed her. She is wearing a robe and slippers. She moves a hand inside her robe and rests it on her chest. I can see a little of her nightgown where the robe doesn't cover. It is frilly pink.

"Please. . .don't let me stop you," she says. "I just wanted to let you know I think you're doing a great job. The president thinks so, too."

I thank her for the compliment. I'm told by Iris that the First Lady doesn't give out many compliments, so I'm happy that she likes my work. Iris talks to me a lot about her relationship with Janey—what she is like to work for, what type of First Lady she is and how she thinks history will treat Janey.

Iris confides to me that she doesn't think Janey really cares how history treats her.

* * *

"Things were rough in the beginning," Iris told me once. "I almost quit soon after I came to work here."

"What happened?"

"Janey can be a real bitch. One time, I wrote a speech for her—I think she was giving a talk the next day before the American Green Growers Association; it was some organization like that. Anyway, she stormed into my office and told me it was the biggest pile of shit she had ever read. She ranted and raved for ten minutes and she threw it down at my feet and ground her heel into it. Then, she kicked the papers and left the room. I have never seen a grown woman throw such a temper tantrum."

"What did you do?"

Iris arched her spine and threw her shoulders back. Her voice grew very defiant.

"I rewrote the speech and when I handed it to Jancy I told her to never use that tone of voice with me again. Janey didn't want to hear that. She pointed a finger at me and said, 'Honey, I'm the First Lady and you're nothing but a poor girl from Mississippi. If you can't do the job, I'll find somebody else.'

"Well, I shouted back at her and she shouted back at me and we carried on that way for about fifteen minutes. Everybody in the East Wing heard us cussing each other, but I wasn't going to back down. No, sir. I didn't raise myself out of the swamps of Blue Pickum and go to college and law school so some snotty white lady could boss me around."

Iris told me that Janey finally gave in. Janey never raised her voice to Iris again and, in fact, she never criticized her work again. Others haven't been so fortunate.

"Hazel is positively frightened of her," said Iris. "The kitchen crew threatened to quit last week because of her and the grounds crew guys filed a complaint with their union."

Iris shook her head. "They aren't strong people," she said. "To get along with Mrs. Robbins, you have to stand up to her. She can be a bully, and the way you get rid of a bully is to not take his shit. I made it clear to Janey early on that I wouldn't take her shit. Now, she respects me.

"The others haven't learned that, yet. I guess they never will. Do you know what Van Buren told me?"

"What?"

"Her Secret Service detail hopes that somebody takes a shot at her."

I'm shocked to hear that.

"Oh!" Iris said, "They don't want to see her dead, but they wouldn't mind seeing her wounded. They hope the bullet hits her in a place that hurts a lot and takes a long time to heal."

Iris laughed at that.

* * *

"I saw you arrive for work a few minutes ago," Janey says. "I heard a loud engine and when I looked out the window I saw you just pulling up on your motorcycle."

"I hope I didn't wake you," I tell her.

"Oh, I've been up for hours."

Of course, I know that is a lie.

She speaks again.

"I saw everyone surround you; at first I thought they were going to shoot you."

"Me too," I say. "I was pretty scared for a minute. I guess they aren't used to people on motorcycles riding up to the front door of the White House."

Janey walks into the room, sits down on a mahogany chair and crosses her legs. She lets her robe and nightgown part, exposing some thigh. She has nice legs.

She leans forward and starts playing with the pink frilly part of her nightgown again.

"I like motorcycles," she says. "Let's go for a ride."

* * *

Twenty minutes later, I am riding the Triumph south on the Beltway with Janey on the back of the bike. I am not making this up. When she tells me she wants to go for a ride I swallow real hard and I want to ask her whether she is crazy, but you just don't say that to the First Lady of the United States.

So I say, "Pardon me?"

Pardon me?

Well, what would you have said?

"I've been on bikes before," she says. "You wait here, I'll be right back."

She walks out the door. I don't know what to do. The First Lady actually wants to take a ride on my chopped Triumph. How do I say no? The answer is I don't. Still, a thousand thoughts are going through my mind:

Is it OK to do this? I mean, is this going to be OK with the president?

What about the Secret Service? They were ready to shoot me for just riding a motorcycle up the driveway. Cripes, what are they going to do when the First Lady hops aboard?

What if we have an accident and she is killed? I decide that if we have an accident, I better be the one who is killed.

Anyway, I'm thinking all this over and I'm in sort of a red haze. I start stirring a can of Raspberry Sorbet just to get my mind off this immediate problem I have. The Red Room, I decide, looks a lot redder at this moment than I can ever remember it.

"I'm ready, let's go!"

I look up and see Janey. Boy, is she ready. She is wearing a pair of black leather knee-high boots with stiletto heels. She is wearing a pair of skin-tight leather biker pants. Around her waist is a very wide chain belt with the Harley-Davidson logo for the buckle. She has on a black tank top and she is not wearing a bra. She is dragging a black leather jacket on the floor behind her. Cradled under her right arm is a black helmet. She is wearing very black sunglasses and very red lipstick. Her mouth is open and her tongue is sort of playing with her lips.

Since the day I came to work here, I have never seen Janey without her hair tied tightly in a knot behind her head. Now, there is no knot. Her red hair is down to her shoulders and sort of hanging in her eyes. She has thick, sensual eyebrows. I find the look very sexy.

At forty-eight, Janey looks great; she is just as sensuous as her 18-year-old daughter. In both cases, their beauty stems from their age. Jodie has fresh looks: the type of face and figure you see on girls who are young enough not to have to work at being pretty. But Janey has to work at staying young. Upstairs, on the third floor of the White House, there is a small workout room that Janey had installed in a vacant bedroom. She has a stationary bicycle and an aerobics mat up there. She also has a treadmill. Outside, there is a jogging track along the perimeter of the South Lawn, but Janey never uses it. She would never dare allow a news crew to film her while she exercises.

Still, she keeps to a strict regimen and it has helped her fight off the aging process. Right now, dressed in black leather and standing at the doorway of the Red Room, she looks delicious. I want to ask if she owns a shorty Japanese kimono, but I'm afraid she may want to know what I know about shorty Japanese kimonos.

We leave the Red Room.

* * *

I don't know how she does it but we walk out the front door of the White House and I don't see a single Secret Service guy. I kick-start the bike and give it some revs. She climbs aboard in back of me and holds me tight around the chest. I can feel her breasts pressing against my back. We start moving. The guard is still at the gate, but he just waves us through. A minute later we are zooming past Lafayette Square and then we're heading up Sixteenth Street. We enter the Beltway right past Rock Creek Park, then we pick up I-95 and head south. I keep looking in my mirror for some sort of escort: you know, like a car full of Secret Service agents trailing behind us, but I see nothing and no one.

We are on our own.

We ride for hours. In the mid-afternoon I pull off the highway and find a burger stand and we stop to eat. She buys. We're someplace south of Richmond, that's all I know. It's a roadside stand with a twenty-foot statue of a fat chef standing in the parking lot. He is wearing a red plaster apron, but it has seen better days. The red has faded and the plaster is chipped. Also, his pink nose is chipped and somebody has thrown a rock through his chef's hat, leaving a gaping hole. My guess is the hat has been that way since at least the Nixon administration.

A waitress comes over and takes our orders. We tell her two cheeseburgers, two Cokes, two fries. She cracks a wad of pink bubblegum and then disappears into the kitchen and it suddenly dawns on me that neither the waitress nor anyone else in this crummy diner realizes the First Lady of the United States is here.

I'm about to mention this to Janey but she has already left the table and has headed over to the far end of the diner, where I see an old jukebox. You don't see many of them around anymore, but this is an authentic old jukebox with a stack of vinyl 45s inside. Janey leans over the machine and it occurs to me that the First Lady has a nice, tight ass.

She digs into a pocket of her leather pants and finds some change, and then she drops it into the jukebox. She has selected something by Clint Black. He starts warbling about how unfair life is to him. Cripes. Country-and-western music hurts my ears.

She returns just as the waitress brings over the Cokes.

Janey sits down and starts sipping.

"Do you know that right now I'm supposed to be serving tea to the wife of the new ambassador from Sri Lanka?"

She laughs at that and sips some more Coke.

"And then, right after tea, I have to meet with Iris and Hazel to work on my itinerary for the National Governors' Association meeting next week. I don't have anything to do with the governors, but I have to show their spouses around Washington while they're here. That sort of thing really bores me."

She rests her elbows on the table, then lets her chin drop into her palms. She sighs.

"I think I have two press interviews today and I'm also supposed to tape a public service announcement, but I really don't even remember what it's for."

I'm beginning to feel empathy for her. I've decided there is more to Janey than a bitchy lady with money.

"But when you don't show up for your appointments...what will happen? Do you think anybody is going to come out looking for you? Isn't your disappearance going to be on the news?"

"I told Iris to cancel my appointments before we left. She asked me why but I wouldn't say. The White House press corps is in Europe with my husband. We'll be OK."

Well, what the hell. If she isn't worried, neither am I. The food comes and we eat. I'm hungry and she is as well. We don't talk much during the meal. People come in and out of the diner all the time and not a single one of them stops and stares.

Janey, it seems, yearns for freedom and a normal life as much as her daughter. But her daughter failed to find it, probably due to her immaturity. When Jodie was given a taste of freedom she bit off hunks too large to swallow. Jodie drowned in her freedom because at eighteen she simply hadn't learned yet how to swim in it. At forty-eight, Janey is much wiser in these matters. She apparently knows how to succeed where her daughter has failed. Janey decided to have a fling with a house painter this morning. She saw my motorcycle and wanted an adventure. I'm certain that she will know when to end it, when to tell me to turn the bike back north. And when people in the White House ask Janey what she did with her day today, why she canceled tea with the wife of the ambassador from Sri Lanka, I have no doubt that Janey will be able to handle it with her usual panache.

We finish eating. "Ready to go?" I say. She nods and we leave the diner.

* * *

We keep heading south. Soon, we're in North Carolina. Tobacco fields line the highways. Black faces look up; the pickers are startled by the noise of the Triumph's nasty engine as we zoom along. By late in the day we have crossed over into South Carolina. We leave the highway again and stop for more burgers. This diner also has a jukebox. Coincidence? Or has Janey made this trip before? Anyway, Janey finds the jukebox and plays some more tunes. We finish eating. "We should find a place for the night," she says. I tell her that's a good idea.

We discover a motel about three miles from the diner. It is a strip motel with about two-dozen rooms. A burned-out neon sign over the office says "Vacancy." Janey waits by the bike while I pay the guy in the office fifty dollars for the room. He is a short, fat turd smoking a putrid cigar and watching cable TV. It is an episode from the old Gomer Pyle TV series, playing on one of those retro cable channels. He gives me a couple of towels.

Janey is an aggressive lover. We embrace as soon as I lock the door of our room and, seconds later, we are coupling on the bed. We nearly tear each other's clothes off. I'm just guessing, but it's my bet the First Lady of the United States of America has a hell of an orgasm.

* * *

We both sleep late; it's past noon when I open my eyes. Janey has come to me three times overnight and it's all I can do to keep up with her. After the second time, she tells me that before tonight, she hadn't had an orgasm in something like twenty years.

And not only that, but she tells me that she and Abe have had sex five times in the last four years. Once was the night of the New Hampshire primary, which was the first primary that Abe won on his way to the nomination. Once was the night of the New York primary, which was when Abe sewed up the nomination. Once was the last night of the Democratic National Convention, which is when Abe gave his acceptance speech. Once was on the night of the election. And once was the night of the inauguration.

"Abe saves himself for big occasions," she sighs.

She snuggles close to me, burrowing her head in my chest. She takes a nibble.

"Ouch!" I protest.

She giggles.

I have some questions.

"The night of the inauguration. . .did you do it in the White House?"

Janey shakes her head.

"Our luggage hadn't arrived yet," she says. "We were still living in a hotel."

I can see why Janey is starved for some passion. At forty-eight, she still has a healthy sexual appetite, but she is frustrated by her inability to lure her husband into bed. She tells me that Abe is a lousy lover.

"He has no idea how to be tender; he has no concept of what a woman wants," she says.

"What do you mean?"

"He bangs away at me as though I'm a piece of red meat. To him, sex is just another opportunity to be president."

* * *

We make love once more, then shower and we're back on the road. By nightfall, we have made Florida. We leave the highway and find a bar in St. Augustine. The name of the bar is the Blue Horizon, and it's a shot-and-beer joint. It is packed with poor white trash. We find a table and order some beers. When we left Washington, we dressed for January. We are now in Florida and it's more like April. The beers are yellow and cold. They taste good. There is already shit-kickin' country music playing on the jukebox, so I guess that makes Janey happy. The cigarette smoke is thick inside the Blue Horizon. I can smell some dope burning. Janey drains her beer quickly and orders another. She has dribbled beer down the front of her tank top.

"Nobody knows me here," she says. "Nobody in here watches the news, reads the papers, browses the Internet or really gives a shit about who is President and who is First Lady. At best, I'd think half of them could name the president."

Janey seems so at ease here, as though she belongs. This is the daughter of a rich man? This is Janey Goldwick Robbins, the consummate American princess who never knew a day's work in her life? The same Janey Robbins who was born to money and married to power?

I want to ask her whether I'm the first house painter she has seduced and taken to a white trash bar in Florida, but she takes my hand and makes me stand up.

"Let's dance," she says.

There is a slow dance playing on the jukebox – Color My World by Chicago. A half-dozen couples are pressed together on the dance floor. We join them. Janey holds me close, pulling herself into me. I'm not much of a dancer, but I do my best to keep in time to the music. Somehow, I don't think that is important to the First Lady; all I think she wants now is to be held.

* * *

We find our table again and order some more beers. Suddenly, a scuffle breaks out behind Janey. Two men are fighting. One man lands a lucky punch and sends the other sprawling. The loser leaves his feet and crashes into Janey, who in knocked to the floor.

Now, if this happens in Washington, a dozen Secret Service agents suddenly appear and that's the end of the story. But we're not in Washington; we're at the Blue Horizon in St. Augustine, Florida, and the Secret Service doesn't know the First Lady is in a shit-kickin' bar with a house painter. Janey doesn't have the Secret Service with her here, she has only me.

So she gets her ass knocked to the floor and, of course, she picks this moment to remember that she is the bitchiest First Lady in the history of the Republic.

"Hey, asshole, watch your fat butt," she says to the guy who just knocked her to the floor.

The guy is big. He is well over six feet tall and he's got a lot of muscles and a belly hanging over his belt. He doesn't have any hair on his head, but he does have a thick, untrimmed mustache. I'm sure he drives truck. He gives Janey a funny look. Then, he smacks her across the face with the back of his hand.

Then he laughs.

"You son-of-a-bitch!" Janey screams.

A tiny dot of red blood has appeared below Janey's bottom lip.

The guy raises his hand again.

As I said, the Secret Service isn't here now. There's only me, so it's me who has to protect the First Lady. I sure wish I had an Uzi, but I don't.

He swings to punch Janey, but I react quickly and grab his hand. I yank it behind him, which twists his shoulder and hurts him a whole lot. I know it must hurt because he winces.

It also makes him madder. He turns to face me and with his free hand reaches out for me. The gorilla grabs a piece of my shirt and starts pulling me toward him, but I move quickly again and knee him in the balls. He doesn't like this either.

He grabs his groin and lets a gust of air escape from his lungs. That's when I let him have a big roundhouse right. I knock the bastard right off his feet, and as he's falling to the ground I see some white teeth and splatters of red blood come out of his mouth. He hits the floor of the bar with a thud. I walk over and stand over him for a moment. Then, I give him a kick in the ribs.

I look up, and every eye in the bar is on us. I look back down at the trucker. He is trying to push himself up from the barroom floor. I give him another kick in the ribs and he goes sprawling again.

Not a bad bit of fighting for a house painter!

I grab Janey by the hand and we're out the door and back on the road within seconds. We ride for about an hour and don't stop until we're positive that nobody followed us. We find a secluded patch of beach and park. Then, we make love in the dunes.

That night we sleep on the beach.

* * *

We are up and riding again at sunrise. Janey tells me she wants to go back to Washington now. We ride all day and stay in a North Carolina motel that night. Again, she is insatiable and I try my best not to be the president. We get an early start again the next day and by noon I have the Triumph on the Beltway. I ask Janey whether she wants me to drop her at the White House. She says no, that I am to take her to a friend's house in Chevy Chase. She gives me directions and I find it easily. It is a very expensive Victorian surrounded by about a hundred acres. I recognize it immediately. It is, of course, the home of Julia and Hector Ramirez, which is the last job I did before the White House. I know Julia and Janey are good friends and that Janey can use the place to clean up and call the White House for a limousine. I'm also sure Julia will keep her mouth shut.

So I drop Janey off and head for home. I have been away from the job for nearly the whole work week and I'm way behind, but I'm too tired to pick up a brush. I go home and sleep for the rest of the day, and then I sleep all night, too. The next morning, I'm on the job early. I finish a whole wall in Raspberry Sorbet when I hear somebody say, "Well, hello stranger."

It's Iris.

"Uhh…hullo Iris," I answer.

I hope she doesn't ask a lot of questions.

She walks in and sits down. She smiles.

"You know," she says. "Funny things been have happening around here ever since you started painting the White House."

"That so?"

She nods.

I tell her I have no idea what she could mean.

* * *

Finally, I finish the Red Room. Good, because I can't stand all that red. What's next? The Blue Room, of course.

You have to know, though, that the Blue Room isn't blue. It's off-white, sort of a Sun Shadow, according to my samples. But most everything else in the Blue Room is blue—the draperies, the upholstery on the furniture, the carpet, the wallpaper border around the wainscoting. It's all blue. It's a big oval room and it's going to take a lot of paint. It's also going to be a ladder job, because it has high ceilings. Cripes.

Iris and I decide to keep the off-white look for the room, because we like the contrast of blue against white. We break out the samples, and this time we call Hazel in to help. Hazel likes Albemarle Sound, Plymouth Square, Quaker Hill Frost and Stony Point. My picks are Clear Opal, One Step for Man, Aquarium Quartz and Bright Star. Iris votes for Cocoa Seeds, Sandy Oasis, Beach Basket, Vanilla Custard, Lambswool and Baby's Smile.

We argue back and forth for the better part of an hour. Finally, Iris convinces me that Vanilla Custard is the best choice. Hazel goes along with us because she doesn't tend to be the argumentative type.

So it is decided: Vanilla Custard will be our selection for the walls of the Blue Room. We decide the trim should be painted Lambswool, which is a whiter white than Vanilla Custard. We think it will work and we are happy with our choices.

That afternoon, I stop by the paint store and tell them to mix up a dozen gallons of Vanilla Custard.

I also pick up some more samples, because I'm going to need them to show my ex-wife Nancy.

The Vanilla Custard Room

I intend to do a good job on the Blue Room. I quickly learn that Vanilla Custard is a wise choice. As soon as I roll it on, I can tell it will offer a sharp contrast to the blue curtains, the blue upholstery, the blue wallpaper trim and the rest of the blue in the room. Iris comes by for a look and agrees.

The Blue Room has a very high ceiling—I'd guess twenty feet or so. That means I have to climb a ladder. I don't like this because sometimes I suffer from vertigo when I'm up on ladders. Anyway, I can't hire a kid to do the stuff on the ladder because of the red tape over the security clearance, so I have to do the work on the ladder myself.

The chandelier hangs from a majestic central medallion that is going to receive a coat of Lambswool. I have brought a very tall stepladder with me today and set it up under the medallion. I scale the rungs and as soon as I am close to the medallion I can tell that it is going to take some scraping. There is some loose paint hanging down and it has to come off before I can apply a coat of Lambswool.

I take my scraper and wire brush out of the pocket of my painter's pants and start working on the medallion and pretty soon I start taking the loose paint off in nice big flakes. While I'm doing this, I'm trying hard not to look down at the floor because, as you know, I have a vertigo problem. Still, you can't work fifteen or twenty feet off the floor without occasionally glancing down, which I do, and wouldn't you know it but I am hit with a spell of vertigo.

Painting the White House

Things start spinning and suddenly I feel woozy and nauseous. I reach up and grab a decorative knob in the shape of a puma head that is protruding from the ceiling medallion. I close my eyes and soon the vertigo passes. I give it a few more seconds and then open my eyes again, being sure to keep my eyes up or at least level because I do not want to give myself another spell all over again.

I look up at the ceiling. I notice my hand is still clutching the puma head and, in fact, I have pulled the knob away from the medallion. The puma head seems to be attached to a trap door, which is part of the medallion. It has been very cleverly fashioned so that the crack around the trap door blends into the medallion. If you aren't looking for the door, you would never find it unless, of course, you find it accidentally, which I have just done.

Anyway, I pull the trap door all the way open and poke my head up through the opening. There is a crawl space above the ceiling; it is very dark but there is just enough light to see. I hoist myself into the crawl space.

It is very weird up here.

There isn't enough room to stand, so I have to crouch down low. The bottom of the crawl space is made up of smooth black and white tiles set down in a checkerboard fashion. Perhaps, at one time in the life of the White House, this was the floor for the story above me. And then, during one of the renovations, a new floor was built above it but they left the old tile floor here. People who live in old houses find little surprises like this all the time.

I start moving on my hands and knees, feeling my way around. There is some light up here, but not much, and soon I am better able to see. My pupils have widened and my eyes have dark-adapted, which helps. A lot of people don't know it, but you really can see in the dark as long as you give your eyes enough time to adjust.

Now that I can see a little better, I take my first good look around. The crawl space seems to be as wide as a football field with the checkerboard tiles sprawling out on all sides. Ahead and behind me the checkerboard pattern continues, with the black and white tiles seemingly ending at the horizon. It appears as though it goes on for miles, but of course I know that can't be. I crawl forward some more and soon realize that there is now enough room for me to stand. I'm a bit surprised by this, but I rise to my feet and start walking. It feels good to be off my hands and feet; they were starting to ache.

The checkerboard seems to go on forever, but my guess is that it's an optical illusion. Occasionally, I look behind and see a square of yellow light shining through the floor—that is the opening for the trap door. It is wise that I have left it open, because who knows how lost you can get around here?

I walk for what seems like hours. Everywhere, I see black and white tile squares beneath me and, incredibly, they are above me as well. The ceiling appears to be forty or fifty feet high. Off in the distance the tiles appear as though they meet at the horizon.

My feet hit the tiles hard and my steps echo as I walk: with each step I take, I hear a *clack-clack-clack-clack-clack*. The noise is a bit unnerving and irksome, but what can I do?

Eventually, I start noticing a change in the black and white tiles. They are no longer square; instead, each one has taken on a slightly different geometrical shape. They seem to be forming parallelograms, and after I walk a bit longer I notice that they are set down in a circular pattern. I follow the tiles into what has become a vortex and at the center of the vortex I find an opening. I kneel down and lean over the opening; I can tell I am looking down into a vertical tube. When I take a closer look, I discover a ladder fixed to a side of the tube.

One final glance back. I make sure I can still see the yellow rays of sunlight from the Blue Room cascading through the trap door opening. It is off in the distance, but clearly it is still there.

I spin around, drop my feet into the tube and begin my descent. Hand over hand I go. As I'm sure I've told you many times, I don't particularly like ladders but I feel no sense of vertigo coming on here. In fact, at times—and I'm sure I can't explain this—I'm not even certain I'm climbing down. Sometimes, it feels as though I am climbing up the ladder. . .and then down again. . .and then up again. Did I say it was weird up here? And then, just when I think I know whether I'm going up or coming down, my inner ear tells me that I'm going neither up nor down, but that I am moving forward as if I'm crawling along on my hands and knees over railroad ties. I am tempted to let go of the ladder rungs, to see what would happen, but I'm afraid I'll fall if I do that. So I hold on tightly, and I continue my descent. . .or ascent. . .or whatever it is I'm doing.

Painting the White House

This seems to go on for an hour or two, although I can't really be sure how long I've been on the ladder. I glance at my watch, but I notice it has stopped running. There is no day or night here, only black and white.

I think often of turning back, but since I have come this far I decide to push on. There must be a bottom to this tube somewhere.

Occasionally, I feel a new motion, as if the ladder is swaying back and forth. It isn't much of a motion; just a hint, a gentle nudging that I can feel more in my stomach than anywhere else. I have the feeling that the tube is under the stress of gravity; that there is a compression, a tension and a bending of the tube. The White House has had trouble with such stresses in the architecture before: in 1948, Harry Truman felt the floor in the upstairs living quarters vibrate occasionally. He brought in some engineers to look the place over and they concluded that the White House was about to collapse. They gutted the whole building then, leaving nothing up but the outside sandstone walls. Inside, they razed everything and built a new frame out of steel I-beams, then they replaced the rooms pretty much in their original design. I'm wondering whether the 1948 renovation had anything to do with the creation of Checkerboardland. Is it a reach to imagine that when the renovators gutted the inner floors, they breached some type of time-space warp? Perhaps they opened a continuum to a new dimension. At the end of this tube, will I enter a parallel world? A parallel White House? Physicists have played with these ideas for decades. I give this some thought, but not too much. Physics is not my science; I'm a house painter. I keep climbing.

I have little trouble seeing, but there is not much to look at: just the same black-and-white checkerboard pattern surrounding me. On and on it goes. But soon, I notice something different—a gentle rush of air blowing by me. It is emanating from below. The air is chilly yet refreshing; the more I climb, the more I can feel it.

The air smells sweet. I decide it must be fresh air, which means the wormhole must be ending soon. I am correct about that. I take a few more steps on the ladder and discover I have run out of rungs. I try to find a place to rest my feet, but I find myself kicking air. I let my feet dangle. At first I am frightened, but I soon realize that although I am hanging only by my hands on the last rung of the ladder I am making no great effort to hold on. Newton's laws are apparently being violated at 1600 Pennsylvania Avenue. I take one hand off the ladder and feel around the wormhole below my knee. I discover that the tube curves into a floor. I swing my feet over the lip of the wormhole, hoist myself out of the tube and, miraculously, I am sitting on another black-and-white tile floor. I stand up, push the wrinkles out of my clothes and look around.

I see the tile floor has formed a vortex with me at the center. Have I just gone around in a circle? It doesn't seem possible, and yet here is everything as I left it a short time ago.

Off in the distance, I see a square of light breaking the black-and-white pattern. I begin walking toward the light.

Once again, it seems to take hours. I have grown weary from all this walking and climbing, but I don't want to take a break until I re-enter the Blue Room.

Something is very funny here. As I draw nearer, I notice the rectangular glow of light at the entrance to the trap door is not yellow. I would describe it more as a Rembrandt Blue or even a King's Navy. I'm wondering if Iris or somebody else on the staff walked by the doorway to the Blue Room, peaked inside and saw the lights on but nobody at work. The Robbins administration has been preaching austerity. It wouldn't surprise me if Iris came along and turned the lights off to save on the White House electric bill. What I am probably seeing, I conclude, are the reflections and shadows from the darkened Blue Room below.

Soon, I arrive at the trap door and the glow is most definitely not yellow. I swing my legs over the side and lower myself down and then I receive the surprise of my life.

The ladder is missing.

"Shit," I murmur.

Now, I've got problems. It is going to be about a twenty-foot drop, but what can I do? Cripes. I think about calling for help, but I'm not sure I'm allowed to be up here. What if some crazy Secret Service agent hears me calling and comes running into the room with his gun drawn? I don't know and I don't want to find out.

I took a sky diving course about ten years ago. I did it to try to shake off my vertigo, but it didn't work so I quit after two lessons. Still, the first thing they teach you is how to land. You would think that when you parachute out of an airplane you just float down nice and easy, but that isn't the case. The landings can be hard sometimes. I remember what the

Painting the White House

instructor told us about rolling forward to break your fall. I remember practicing it. We all had to stand on top of a stone wall that was about ten feet high, and then we had to jump off and roll forward as we hit the ground. It's easy once you practice. Know what? I jumped off that wall a half-dozen times and not once did I hurt myself. Of course, that was a ten-foot drop and this is a twenty-foot drop. Cripes, what can I do?

So I hang down through the trap door opening by my hands and start my body swinging back and forth, and then as I'm swinging forward I let go. I hit the floor hard, but just as I do I tumble forward. This eases the fall, but I still bang around on the floor pretty hard. I jump immediately to my feet and am pleasantly surprised that nothing seems to be broken.

And then, I suddenly notice that I have no idea where I am.

It sure isn't the Blue Room of the White House.

* * *

The walls aren't Vanilla Custard nor is the trim Lambswool. The colors are more like charcoal black; closer, I think, to a Husky Blue or an Iron Horse. They aren't quite black, but they are almost black. The curtains are yellow. So is the upholstery on the furniture. The wallpaper border is yellow, as well. It is a terrible room, the walls and ceiling are nearly black, the furnishings are yellow. This must be a joke. It occurs to me that I may have been gone from the job for hours while I was wandering around on checkerboard tiles. Perhaps, Van Buren and Webster have come along, found the place empty and painted the Blue Room in hideous shades of yellow and black as a joke.

I quickly dismiss that notion. Secret Service guys have absolutely no sense of humor. And besides, I don't think anyone on staff here would ever conceive of such a joke. Certainly, they could lose their jobs.

All this thinking has puzzled me. I find the door and leave.

The hallway is as dark as the walls in the room I have just left. There are lights shining from incandescent fixtures overhead, but they do not do a good job of illuminating my way. In fact, the bulbs seem to be giving off a dark blue glow. It is a cool light and suddenly I discover that I am chilly. I shiver.

Soon, I see what I think is a familiar door. It is the entrance to the Red Room, which as you know I have just finished painting Raspberry Sorbet. I enter and, again, I am surprised to find that it is not quite the room I thought it was. It is blue in here; a different blue than I've been seeing in the hallways, but there is no question the Red Room is now blue. I would describe the walls in the Red Room as a lighter shade of blue, perhaps a cyan. Yes, definitely cyan.

I painted the trim in the Red Room deep gray. Now, it is white again—or, almost white.

I sit down on one of the cyan chairs and attempt to think this all out. Obviously, I am not in the same White House I was in earlier today. Everything is opposite. Painters know a lot about color, and they know that cyan is the opposite of red, yellow is the opposite of blue and black is the opposite of white. I haven't been to the Lincoln Bedroom yet, but I have no doubt that I will not find the Buffalo Bill green that I applied there a few weeks ago, but instead I will find magenta walls. Magenta is the opposite of green. It is similar to a fluorescent shade of red, the type of red you would see in a child's crayon box.

I stare at the cyan that surrounds me and it occurs to me that I am not sitting in a room of pure cyan. I'm sure I know the reason. In the other White House, I use variations on primary colors. That means I will never find, for example, pure cyan here in the Red Room. It will be slightly different, just as Raspberry Sorbet is slightly different from pure, basic red.

I rise from the chair and walk over to the floor-to-ceiling window that overlooks the White House lawn. Outside, I see acres and acres of magenta grass and tall, leafless off-white magnolia trees dotting the landscape. I thrust open the Palladian windows and lean out, then twist my head so that I am looking back at an exterior sandstone wall. No surprise, but the White House is now the Black House. It makes me shiver. I close the windows and leave the room.

I wander the charcoal-blue hallways, trying to make sense of it all. That is impossible, I'm sure. I turn a corner and, ahead of me, I see a green settee off to the side of the corridor. A woman is lounging in the settee, smoking. She is barely illuminated by the cold light above her head. It is Jodie and she is wearing her kimono. I see black lotus blossoms stitched into the kimono now. Her skin tone is dark blue, her curly hair almost white. She has white eyebrows and cyan lips. She is picking at a cuticle on her toenail. She looks bored. She glances at me as I stumble by, but shows no emotion. I want to talk to her, but I can't move my lips. I approach another corner and glance back, but she is gone now. The settee remains.

Hey! I told you that this was, like, really weird.

I walk on, occasionally glancing in rooms. The other White House has square rooms, rectangular rooms, even oval rooms. Not this White House. The rooms are obscene jokes on geometry: none of the walls are parallel, none of the corners form ninety-degree angles, none of the ceilings are flat. Some of the ceilings appear to rise for stories and stories; some of the floors seemingly dip so low that they fall into the earth. Some of the walls are curved, some are completely circular. There is more order and exactness in a house of mirrors than there is in here.

And everywhere, I see colors that clash, colors that splash into each other, colors that hurt the eyes, colors that are simply indescribable, colors that I don't think you'll find on any painter's chip or, for that matter, in any spectrum in this universe.

I stumble on, entering the Lincoln Bedroom, which I have painted Buffalo Bill. Now the walls are off-magenta. I enter the room and find a woman sitting cross-legged on the bed. Her back is to me. She is holding an ornamental hand mirror near her face. The mirror is round; its handle is glossy black opal and it is carved into fancy curlicues. I look closer at the handle, and I can see nudes entwined in each other's limbs. The woman is using the mirror to primp her hair, which is jet black and falls around her shoulders. Her skin is very white, about as white as I've ever seen skin. Albino, even. She is wearing white lace.

I take a step closer to the old bed. I can see her face in the mirror, now. It is Janey.

I go to her.

* * *

I wake up. How long have I slept? I can't answer that. Through the window, I see the sky is black, but what does that mean? Is it nighttime outside? Who can say for sure?

Janey has left. Was she ever here?

I look around the Lincoln Bedroom. The walls are still magenta, not Buffalo Bill green. I leave and wander some more. Soon, I enter a long corridor; I think it is the Cross Hall, which has a red carpet. Of course, the carpet is cyan now.

The Yellow Oval Room is next. I enter the great room and find it is now mostly blue. I find Warren Adams hanging from the chandelier. This time I am too late. He is already dead. The body sways in the breeze, his corpse throwing a white shadow on the dark blue walls. I can hear a creaky sound: obviously, the weight of his body is straining the chandelier. His face is contorted, his hair jet black, his black eyes bulge from their sockets. Cyan blood is dripping on the floor. I feel sick and wonder why nobody has cut him down. He is hanging too high for me to reach. I find my painter's knife in my pocket and know it has a sharp blade but, alas, I have no ladder. What can I do? I leave poor opposite-Warren hanging there. I guess, in this world, he didn't get to be president, either.

Soon, I am back in the Blue Room. This time, I find the wormhole on the floor. I crawl back in and begin scaling the ladder. I travel for hours. Once again, I am surrounded by smooth tiles, but I can tell they are not the same tiles that I saw before. No longer are they black and white. Now they are white and black.

I can see the difference.

* * *

On my way home from the White House I stop at Nancy's apartment. Franklin isn't yet home from work. I'm not sure why I called Nancy the day before and said I was coming over. I certainly hadn't given her much thought since our divorce. Also, I can't say I really have that much of an interest in exchanging ideas about linguistic anthropology with her. And, deep down, I know she doesn't want to have her apartment painted. But I call and she tells me to come over because she doesn't have any classes that afternoon.

"Where do you live?"

"On N Street. You know the address, silly, you used to live there."

"You never moved?"

"Why move?"

I am stunned by this news, but I can think of no reason for her not to be living in the old apartment.

Anyway, I head over to Georgetown with some paint samples. Nancy lives near the grounds of the U.S. Naval Observatory, which is where the vice president lives, you know. I knock on the door and Nancy answers.

Well, she may be forty but she looks pretty much how I remembered her at twenty—same auburn hair, same upturned nose, same long legs, same fondness for tight sweaters.

Painting the White House

Nancy smiles and invites me in. She leads me into the kitchen and tells me she is going to brew a kettle of herbal tea.

The apartment is the same, too. The furniture looks very familiar, and I conclude that Franklin and Nancy have added virtually nothing to the decor since I moved out twenty years ago.

And, as you know, twenty years ago Nancy and I were still destitute college students. We furnished the apartment by going to flea markets and junk sales and second-hand stores. I'm sure the Louis XVI chair in the Yellow Oval Room that Warren stood on when he tried to hang himself cost fifty times more than Nancy and I spent furnishing our entire apartment twenty years ago. But at the time, our furniture fit our space, just as the furniture in the Blue Room fits that space.

We sit at the kitchen table. I remember this table because I'm the one who found it along a highway one day. I was working for Blackie's crew back then and we were doing a job in Silver Spring. I saw it along Route 410, stopped and rolled it into my truck.

It had originally been a spool for heavy industrial electrical cable. We needed a kitchen table then and I thought this could do in a pinch. Nancy loved it. She painted it in flashy acrylic reds, blues and yellows, and then she put a vase of pink and yellow flowers in the middle.

Nancy and Franklin are still using it as a kitchen table, after all these years. The vase looks familiar as well, although I am certain she has changed the flowers.

"I see you still have the table," I say.

She nods.

I glance around the apartment some more. There is a set of bookshelves against one wall. It is made up of bare wooden planks sandwiched between concrete construction blocks. Nancy's record collection is stacked in some milk crates—she still has her old black vinyl LP's. There are some Grateful Dead black-light posters tacked to the wall behind a red and green bean-bag chair. The plastic covering of the green bean-bag chair is torn, and someone (Franklin?) has repaired it with a swath of silver duct tape.

"You haven't changed a thing," I say.

Most of all, she hasn't changed the walls. I recall it all now: the weekend before I came home from work early and caught Nancy in bed with Franklin, I painted the whole apartment. I remember doing the living room in watered-down burnt orange—Blackie had some left over from a job.

The paint is still there. Of course, after twenty years, it has faded in some spots, cracked in some places and, overall, it has picked up a coat of fingerprints, grime and scuff marks. All over, I see tiny nail holes in the walls: places where picture frames have been hung and moved.

These walls are wounded. They have become sick with neglect. As a painter, it gives me pain to see people treat their walls this way.

My mind is racing in a thousand different directions. I don't know why I am here: certainly, I have told myself that I do not want to paint Nancy's apartment, and yet, I do want this job because I want the challenge of helping these walls heal. I know, also, that I will be able to charge a lot of money. I take a sip of herbal tea.

* * *

It doesn't take long to fill in each other on our lives. I tell her I have a good painting business going, that I never married again, and that right now I'm painting the White House which, I can tell, impresses her. She tells me that she married Franklin shortly after our divorce, that they have no children (his fault, she implies), that she teaches at George Washington and that she has written two books on linguistic anthropology and is now researching her third.

"It's going to be about kinesics," she says.

"Kinesics? I didn't know that was your field."

"It's really isn't, but I've gotten interested in it lately and I think I can do enough research to write a book."

Kinesics is the study of non-verbal communication. It deals with postures of the body and the movement that body parts play in communicating. Many people move parts of their body while they speak and never realize that they may be conveying their message that way as much as they are conveying it through spoken language. A facial expression, for example, could tell a lot about whether the speaker is angry, sad, happy, content or whatever.

Actually, I'm over-simplifying the science. Kinesics is a very difficult field to study and understand. Imagine, for example, the researcher who spends her life trying to understand the meaning of a smile and then finding out that in another culture, in another part of the world, a smile could have a totally different meaning.

Painting the White House

I studied kinesics as an undergraduate. I found it boring. Anyway, Nancy tells me a little more about the book, but I can't say I really have that much interest. To the average house painter, kinesics is a big yawn.

Finally, though, I practice some kinesics and cock an eyebrow at her.

"You know, when Franklin told me that you wanted to see me because you want your apartment painted, I didn't believe him."

She looks at me, puzzled.

I smile and lean forward. The fragrance of herbal tea rising from my cup is sweet and steamy.

"I thought you wanted to see me because you want to fuck."

"Oh!" she says. "We can still do that if you want."

Nothing like good old verbal communication.

* * *

It takes me two weeks to finish the Blue Room. This is much more time than I have planned to spend on the room, but the going is slow because I take a few more trips into Checkerboardland, which I have taken to calling the crawl space. Each time I go into the other White House, I come back weary, drained and uninspired. So after a week of this, I resolve to stay away from the checkerboard and concentrate on the Blue Room.

Finally, I finish and move on to the next room, which is the Roosevelt Room.

I am delighted the Roosevelt Room is next on the schedule because it is small and it will be simple to do. I am, after all, way behind schedule, but by painting the Roosevelt Room next I should be able to catch up. In fact, there are some small, simple rooms on the schedule for the next few weeks. That's good. That way, it will look as though a lot is getting done because a lot of rooms will be painted in a short period of time. That should keep Iris off my back.

The walls of the Roosevelt Room are painted in a pinkish-orange hue. I think they look OK, but Iris tells me that Janey doesn't like the color. The room is used as a staff meeting room. It has Queen Anne and Chippendale furniture, including a very handsome mahogany breakfront bookcase. There is a cozy fireplace, which is painted in white, and the ceiling is white as well.

Anyway, Iris says that Janey thinks the room is too feminine and she wants a more macho color. There is, after all, a painting of Teddy Roosevelt hanging on the wall showing the big guy in his Rough Rider gear. You can't get any more macho than that.

So Iris and I dive into the chips. We want to keep an earthen color, but we're looking for something a bit browner. I think we need a color that says *"People Who Work in This Room Sometimes Get Down in the Mud."* I tell that to Iris, and she gives me a funny look, but I think she grasps the meaning.

I think Cedar Rust or Chilibean will work in the room. Iris favors Sorrel Horse or Java. We argue back and forth and I prevail with Chilibean, which is a dark brown. We want an earthen trim paint as well for the fireplace, and after talking it over we narrow it down to Weathered Buff and Powderhorn. Powderhorn is a light brown, and that's the color we pick. We decide to leave the ceiling white. That's my suggestion, and I tell Iris that a very bright white will be a good complement to the two earthen colors we have selected for the room. I really want to leave the ceiling white because I know I can save time if I don't have to paint it again. Of course, I don't tell this to Iris.

In any event, she agrees with me. The walls will be Chilibean, the fireplace and trim will be Powderhorn and the ceiling will be white.

I know I can finish the job in three days. If I hurry, two. I am pleasantly surprised, though, when I manage to finish painting the Roosevelt Room in one day.

Of course, when I start work on the room I have no way of knowing I will have lots of help.

The Chilibean Room

Tom Thatcher met Abe Robbins in law school. They took some classes together and worked on the law review at the same time, but they were never really close friends. Still, when Abe decided to run for president he made a list of people to contact for help and placed Tom high on the list. Abe wanted Tom in the campaign because he remembered his old school mate's doggedness and determination as well as his intelligence, his ability to find solutions to knotty problems and his steely resolve to always win. Also, though, by the time Abe Robbins was putting his campaign team together, Tom was not exactly an unknown in political circles. At the time, he was the Democratic Party chairman of St. Petersburg, Florida, and was widely considered one of the most powerful political wheels in Florida politics.

Over the years, Tom Thatcher had made his share of judges, mayors, legislators and congressmen. He was on a first-name basis with Florida's governors and senators, all of whom owed him favors. When Abe Robbins added up all the things he needed to win the presidency, the Florida primary was one of them and that meant Tom Thatcher would be vital.

For his part, Tom was delighted when his old law school classmate called, and quickly accepted Abe's offer to head the Florida campaign. Florida was important. On the political calendar, it comes right after New Hampshire. Abe knew that if he won New Hampshire, he would be considered a serious candidate for the presidency. If he won Florida, he would be the front-runner.

Tom went into action. He called in every political chit, he tapped every source for money that he knew, he called every newspaper editorial writer in his Rolodex, and he crisscrossed the state a dozen times. He also delivered Florida big for Abe, and since Abe had, indeed, won the New Hampshire primary, it meant that now Abe was at the head of the Democratic field.

On election night, at the victory party in Miami Beach, Abe summoned Tom to his penthouse suite in the Ritz Plaza Hotel. Tom found Abe reclining on a Cherokee red giltwood sofa decorated with red and white tapestries of Jazz Age dancers. His shoes were off, his tie loosened; but he was sober, excited and full of verve. In contrast, Tom was exhausted; he had been campaigning since dawn, crisscrossing southern Florida, working the phones, leaning on party leaders to turn out the vote for Abe.

It had been the most exciting day of his life and it was ending in a penthouse suite high above Miami Beach. Across the room, Tom could see the French doors leading out to the seaside balcony, and beyond the balcony he saw thousands of incandescent lights lining Collins Avenue. On one side of Collins Avenue was the Atlantic Ocean, on the other side the remaining forty-eight states Abe had yet to win.

Tom felt challenged. He was weary from his long day of campaigning, but he was not going to let his exhaustion get in the way of savoring Abe's Florida triumph. At the moment, Tom considered himself at the center of the universe. He wanted to go down to the ballroom to drink champagne and dance with women, to eat fatty food and give press interviews, to laugh at the competition and make boasts that he knew no one would believe.

He smiled at his candidate. Abe looked fit, flushed and not at all tired. He had started the day before seven, greeting voters at a polling place in Jacksonville. He worked his way down south, ending at a late afternoon rally in the Art Deco district. There was a short nap before dinner, and then some network TV interviews down in the Ritz Plaza's ballroom in time to make the six o'clock news.

And now, with victory in Florida at hand, Tom found Abe full of zest.

"Tom, we really kicked some ass today," said Abe.

Tom Thatcher sat down in a giltwood chair that matched the sofa. He had been involved in a lot of campaigns since moving to Florida. He had

Painting the White House

made a lot of men into leaders and had been on hand for many victory celebrations. But he had never helped put a president over.

His girth sank into the soft cushion of the giltwood chair, creasing the cartoonishly long legs of the jazz dancers. He liked the feel of the chair and the room; he liked the feel of being at the center of power, at the center of it all. Sure, he had power here in Florida, but that was in St. Petersburg. It was a minor-league city all the way, and Tom knew it. Washington would be different. The White House, the presidency...Tom thought about it and knew he could never go back to St. Petersburg.

Tom glanced at a framed print hanging on the wall behind the sofa where Abe was sitting. It was a poster-sized reprint of a photograph of Josephine Baker, the jazz dancer. Josephine was posing in a costume of beads and sequins and feathers and very little else. The print was selenium-toned, giving it a purplish tint. Josephine appeared to be laughing hysterically in the picture, thoroughly enjoying the display she was making of herself. The picture was framed in an ellipse of black Bakelite, buffed to a hard gloss.

Tom wanted the same picture for his office. He wanted his office to be in the White House. Of course, his office would be in the West Wing.

So when Abe asked Tom to stay with the campaign for the year, to become a part of the braintrust, Tom quickly agreed. For the next nine months, Tom slept four hours a night and never in the same hotel room two nights in a row. He visited all fifty states—even Alaska and Hawaii—but most of his time was spent in Ubers, banquet halls or storefront campaign offices. It all paid off. Abe was elected and Tom was invited into the administration. At first, Tom wanted to be chief of staff, but Abe said he needed a Capitol Hill guy for that and Tom simply had no experience there. Tom understood, but he was a little hurt that he wouldn't be named to the top job. Warren Adams won the job. Tom despised Warren Adams.

Instead, Abe offered Tom the job of "Director of Policy and Planning." Abe said Tom would be in on all the major policy decisions in the administration and he would certainly be a part of formulating them. He could hire a staff, have an office in the West Wing and be a major influence on the direction of the government.

Tom accepted. He closed his law office in St. Petersburg, which was no big deal because Tom had few clients and most of them were small central Florida cities and other municipalities that had retained him as a solicitor. They were all political plums he had won over the years as head of St. Petersburg politics.

He had no wife or children to bring to Washington. He had never married. He had never even owned a house. Since leaving law school, Tom had rented a small St. Petersburg apartment, but he hardly did more than sleep there. He hired a housekeeping service to keep it clean and a laundry service to do his wash. He ate most of his meals in restaurants, a fact that had led to his corpulent profile. When he wasn't at his law office, he was usually at St. Petersburg Democratic headquarters. Politics was his whole life; he never had any other interest. He had no hobbies. He played golf, but only because politicians play golf; truth was, he was a terrible golf player. His participation in the St. Petersburg Bar Association was minimal, except that nearly every senior member of the group had approached him at one time or another about becoming a judge. He never dated. Tom was simply in too much of a hurry to meet women. He never attended a social occasion that didn't have something to do with Florida politics and, as such, the only women he knew were politicians.

He did enjoy imported cigars. He usually could be seen chewing on the end of one in the proverbial smoke-filled rooms. When he couldn't smoke them because of no smoking laws, he just chewed on them.

When Tom arrived in Washington he was determined to become a player in the White House. Abe gave him a budget for a staff and he responded by hiring five of the brightest young people he could find.

Tom knew he needed a good staff, mainly because he knew his own limitations and knew he had never really been at home with the issues. Tom had always been the consummate political animal, no question about that, but he knew very little about how the government actually worked. He never drafted candidates based on their ideas; what was important to Tom was how they sold their ideas to the voters. It never mattered what Tom thought about an issue because Tom's name never appeared on the ballot. In essence, then, Tom Thatcher never took a position because he never had to take a position.

Tom knew politics, for sure, but he had no politics of his own.

And Tom knew that wouldn't do in the White House.

* * *

For once in his life, Tom Thatcher put politics aside and hired on the basis of merit rather than political connections. He knew that if he filled his staff with hacks and straphangers, it would reflect on him and his standing in the West Wing would drop. Tom considered himself in competition with Warren Adams and he was damned if Warren was going to be the first among equals in this administration.

So Tom scoured the college campuses, looking for the best and the brightest. He wanted graduate students and law students. He wanted young people with no families because he intended to work them around the clock. He wanted people who never had real jobs before because he didn't want them bringing bad habits they may have learned elsewhere to the White House. He wanted fresh young minds that would provide him with startling ideas which he could throw at Warren Adams and those other bastards on Capitol Hill.

During his months working in the campaign, Tom had been responsible for organizing Robbins for President organizations on college campuses. He called back his local university organizers and asked for names of the schools' brightest prospects. He soon had a list of more than a hundred names. Tom looked over the resumes and shaved that list down to twenty. He interviewed all twenty candidates on the new list and selected five prospects. All five accepted his offers, although he had to cajole a few of them into it.

Tom found Sam Finn at Harvard Law School. He was just finishing up classes and preparing to clerk for a Supreme Court justice when Tom talked him into taking some time off to work in the White House. Although he had never been in a courtroom in his life, Sam knew the law as well as any of his professors and had been looking forward to moving to Washington and working at the Supreme Court. Now, he would still live in Washington only he would be making more money. Tom wanted Sam to be his legal guy.

Tom found Rebecca James at Dartmouth. Rebecca was a graduate student in economics and had just turned in her dissertation when she was approached by Tom. Rebecca was being courted by a dozen Fortune's 500 companies. Tom couldn't offer their salaries to her, but he could sell her on the idea of working in the White House. Rebecca was an expert on statistical analysis. Tom vitally needed somebody who could crunch numbers. He also needed women on his staff.

Luis Calaveras filled the minority slot on Tom's staff. Luis was the computer guy. Tom found him at UCLA. When he was eight years old, Luis built his first Ham radio. When he was twelve years old, he was already writing software. He graduated from college at nineteen and was finishing up graduate school at twenty-one when Tom approached him. Luis told Tom that he already had an offer from Microsoft and planned to take it. Tom dug in his heels and really pushed the idea of serving his country, and finally Luis relented. Tom needed a computer guy and it really helped that he was Hispanic-American as well.

Tom knew he would be dealing with the military a lot, that every general and admiral at the Pentagon would be pushing their pet projects at the White House. Tom wanted an engineer who could look over all those weapons of mass destruction and tell him whether any of them had a chance to work. Tom hired Wayne Marks for that. Wayne was finishing up at Brown. He had already accepted a job at Lockheed when Tom called. Again, Tom pushed patriotism. Wayne agreed, and Tom had his engineer.

The final aide he hired was Polly Morris. Tom found Polly at Princeton where she was a graduate assistant in the political science department. Polly had done some writing for a number of small-circulation liberal political journals. Tom wanted somebody with an expertise in the academic side of politics, somebody who was a pure thinker, somebody who could freelance and be available for any project Tom might come up with. Tom knew that he had four very qualified and capable technocrats on his staff, but he wanted somebody who could see the human side, somebody who knew something more about life than just numbers, statistics and spreadsheets. In her job interview, Polly told Tom that she had been a fine arts major before transferring to political science. Tom knew he had found his fifth aide. Polly was a good fit.

All five of them were at their desks in the White House the morning that Abe Robbins took the oath of office. All five of them were zealously devoted to Tom Thatcher. All five of them worked eighteen-hour days, skipped lunches and usually showed up in the White House on weekends. All five of them brought the type of youthful enthusiasm to the White House that Tom had expected when he hired them.

And I found all five of them, along with Tom Thatcher himself, sitting around the conference table in the Roosevelt Room the morning I showed up with six gallons of Chilibean.

The door is open when I arrive, and I can tell Tom is shouting at them. I don't think he is angry with them, but he is angry at something and they just happen to be in his way at the moment. I'm sure this goes on a lot.

"If he tries it again, I just know the press is going to find out about it," Tom says, shaking his cigar at his aides. The cigar isn't lit, as you know there is no smoking in the White House. He has done a good job, though, of chewing up the end.

He continues: "I don't give a damn if the guy kills himself. In fact, I would like to see Warren Adams kill himself, but I don't want to see him do it while Abe is president, and I certainly don't want to see him do it in the White House."

Everyone in the room nods. I stand silently at the doorway for several more minutes, listening to Tom Thatcher run his staff meeting. No one has noticed me.

"Somebody's got to talk to him and make it clear he can't run around the White House hanging himself from chandeliers," Tom says. "Christ, do you know a couple of reporters have already asked me whether the rumors about Warren's attempted suicide are true?"

Tom shakes his huge head. He is losing his hair.

"Christ," he says again. "If he tries to kill himself again and he fucks up and doesn't die, I'm going to kill him. I'll kick his ass and then I'll strangle him with my bare hands. Christ."

Everyone in the room makes nervous little laughs.

Tom Thatcher certainly is no Warren Adams. In fact, he is the antithesis of Warren. Where Warren is a planner, Tom is a man of action; where Warren is respected for his talent as a negotiator, Tom is feared for his take-no-prisoners commando tactics; where Warren is content to occasionally take a short-term loss if it means a long-term gain, Tom is satisfied with nothing less than a complete scorched-earth victory; where Warren is cerebral, Tom is shallow. And where Warren is suicidal, Tom is homicidal.

I've heard enough. I clank the cans of Chilibean together to announce my entrance and everyone turns in their chairs to face me. I intend to kick them out of the room so that I can start painting. I don't want to fall any further behind than I already am.

"You, painter!" Tom shouts. "You're the guy I want to talk to."

"Uhhh...Me?"

"Yeah, you. Listen, everyone is talking about you, how you may know something about Warren trying to kill himself. Is that true?"

I shake my head.

"C'mon pal, I've heard you may have walked in on him when he was trying to hang himself. Did it happen that way?"

"I don't know what you're talking about."

"Hey, you can talk to me," he says. "If it's true and Warren Adams is suicidal, he needs help. I can help him."

Of course, I know Warren needs somebody's help but I am sure he would prefer it would be somebody other than Tom Thatcher.

I have talked with Warren and understood him, something that Tom Thatcher would never do. I understand what has motivated him to try to kill himself, and although I knew I could never completely comprehend why he would try to take his own life, I have empathy for him. Tom Thatcher has empathy for no one.

No, I decide, knowledge of Warren's attempted suicide would be a dangerous tool in the hands of Tom Thatcher. If Warren Adams wants to tell the president all about it, then that is Warren's business—not mine and not Tom Thatcher's. I decide to keep my mouth shut.

"I heard those rumors, too, and there is nothing to them," I tell Tom. "I spoke with Warren a few weeks ago, but I swear I never saw him try to kill himself. Warren Adams wanted me to come over to his house to price a painting job for him. We talked about it for about ten minutes and I said I would get over when I had the chance. I've been busy here and simply haven't had the opportunity to price his job. Honest, Mr. Thatcher, I never saw Warren Adams try to take his own life."

Well, hell, it isn't the first time anyone has told a lie within these walls.

Tom Thatcher cocks an eyebrow at me. Then, he sticks his cigar in his mouth and starts chewing. They decide to return to their meeting. Luis rises and speaks. I spread dropcloths around the room. I hope they will pick up on the idea that I intend to start painting in here and they will leave, but all six of them just sit around the table and continue their meeting.

Finally, I say, "Excuse me, but I'm going to start painting in here in a few minutes. I really can't work around you. . ."

Tom speaks.

"We're almost done with our meeting. You go ahead and start and we'll be out of here in five minutes."

I shrug and work on. I mix up my first gallon of Chilibean and pour it into a tray. I dip my roller in and start applying it to a wall. I've always been very good at roller work—at keeping a wet edge, which is very important when you do a wall by roller. I defy you to look over my work, here in the White House or any other place I've painted, and tell me whether you see paint streaks or drips in my walls. Sorry, Bubba, but they just aren't there.

To me, the painting part has always been the fun part of painting. They say the secret to painting is ninety percent preparation, and that is true. I pay a lot of attention to that part of the job—spackling and patching the walls first and then cleaning them with tri-sodium phosphate. I also do a lot of taping, especially around ornate woodwork like you see in the White House, but I am quite deft at cutting in and I'm not afraid to go at the slats in a pane window with nothing more than my one-inch brush. Still, I am a dog about preparation, and that is why I think my skills are very much in demand.

But when the preparation is done and the paint is mixed, that is when I really shine. There is something pleasing and relaxing about applying paint to a wall. I think physics may have something to do with it: the wall is flat and the roller is round. They fit together the way yin and yang fit together. They are in balance, as man is in balance with woman, cold is in balance with heat, the sun is in balance with the moon, the sea is in balance with the land.

That's what makes painting so natural: a good painter will bring equilibrium to a room. Anybody who has ever painted a room knows how I feel.

Anyway, I'm working away with my roller and every once in awhile I glance over at Tom and his aides and notice one or more of them looking at me. First, I see that Tom is looking my way, which doesn't surprise me because I still think he doesn't believe my version of the Warren Adams story. I suspect that he wants to talk to me further about it, so I must be on my guard all the time.

Still, Tom isn't the only one looking my way. I notice Polly watching me out of one eye, and Sam is watching me and so is Rebecca and Wayne: not all at once, but they are stealing glances. Only Luis is not paying attention to me, but he is doing the talking so I guess he's concentrating on what he's trying to say.

Suddenly, Tom interrupts Luis.

He points to me.

"That looks like fun," he says.

"This? Fun? This is work."

I roll on some more paint. I don't want to let on to him that it is, indeed, fun. I look over my shoulder, though, and I can tell he is skeptical.

"How can anyone enjoy this?" I say. "This is hard work. . .painting."

I take a step back from the wall and frown.

"This is really poor work I'm doing. I hope you won't tell Janey and Iris how sloppy this is."

Tom jumps to his feet and ambles over.

"I don't think it's sloppy. . .I think it looks like a neat job."

He inspects my work carefully.

"Let me try," he says.

"Oh, I couldn't do that. Janey wouldn't like that. She hired me to do this room and I have to fulfill my contract."

"Janey will never know," he says, and then he turns quickly to look at his aides. They respond with tiny nods.

He reaches into his pocket, pulls out his billfold and peels off a twenty. He shoves it into a pouch in my overalls. I shrug and hand him the roller.

"How do you keep it from dripping?" he asks.

"The paint?"

"Right," Tom says. "The paint."

"No big deal," I answer. "The secret is don't put too much paint on the roller. If you do, you'll put too much paint on the wall and it will drip. Dripping isn't bad if you catch it; it's easy to roll right over a drip. But if you don't catch it, the drip will dry as a drip and it will look awful."

"Show me," he says.

I pick up another roller and dab it into the tray, and then I roll out a sheen of Chilibean onto the wall. I do this a couple of more times, and then the Director of Policy and Planning for the President of the United States dabs his roller into the paint tray as well.

"Be careful," I tell him. "You don't want to get any on your suit."

Tom takes the roller and, naturally, he applies too much paint so when he rolls it onto the wall it makes a mess. I take the roller back and clean

Painting the White House

it up, making sure not to leave any streaks. "You used way too much; you only need about half as much paint on the roller. Try again."

This time he does a better job. He puts just enough paint on the roller and lays a nice even coat on the wall. I give him some direction, telling him to work up and down at an angle—which is accepted painter's practice—and he follows my instructions pretty well. I coach him on keeping a wet edge. He beams, chews on his cigar and keeps looking over at the conference table, smiling like a Cheshire cat. I can tell he's showing off.

"Don't forget to feather the edge and let the roller do the work," I counsel.

His five aides sit silently while Tom paints a wall in the Roosevelt Room. No one suggests they return to work on whatever they are trying to figure out. I stand next to Tom. I want to take the roller back, but he is having so much fun that I don't dare ask.

"Haven't you ever done this before?" I say, at last.

"Nope," he answers as he rolls the paint on. "I always lived in apartments, you know, and the maintenance guys always did this. If I had known how much fun it would be, I would have done it myself."

So I let him go on working, marveling at what I have just created. A life-long apartment dweller, Tom Thatcher has never painted a wall in his life. He has probably never fixed his own toilet, hammered his own nail or even cut his own grass. At the age of forty-seven, Tom has missed out on practicing the fundamental law that provides for a symbiotic relationship between man and his tools.

Soon, I notice that Tom's five aides have surrounded us. They are watching their boss slap paint on the wall. Two of them are even taking notes. I glance at them, but they don't notice me. Instead, they stare at Tom Thatcher painting a wall in the Roosevelt Room.

I know exactly what to do.

I have two extra rollers with me today. I mix up two more gallons of Chilibean and without asking, I hand rollers to Sam and Polly. Sam looks at me with a bit of a puzzled expression. He gingerly dips the roller into the Chilibean and rolls it onto the wall next to Tom. He makes a lot of drips; I am about to correct him when Tom speaks up.

"Asshole!" he shouts. "You're doing it all wrong. Nice, even strokes. . .not too much paint. . .keep a wet edge. . .like this!"

Tom shows Sam how to do it. Meanwhile, Polly bends over and dabs her roller into the paint. She holds the dripping roller up very close to her nose and sniffs it. She wrinkles her nose, and then notices the paint is starting to drip onto her fingers.

"You have to put it on the wall right away or it will do that," I tell her.

She forces a smile, shrugs, and then applies the paint to the wall. I can tell she is a quick study; her first roll goes on very evenly, no drips, no splatters.

I'm out of rollers but I have plenty of brushes. I mix up a couple of gallons of Powderhorn and hand the brushes to Luis, Wayne and Rebecca. I put Rebecca to work on the fireplace and I start Luis and Wayne on the baseboard.

Soon, everybody is working and let me tell you, they are having a great time. They are laughing, talking politics, singing songs, carrying on. They are also slopping up everywhere. It's fortunate I have plenty of dropcloths down to protect the carpet and the furniture. I can't do anything about their clothes. All the men have on dark blue or charcoal suits and by now they have all spilled generous amounts of Powderhorn and Chilibean on themselves. Polly and Rebecca have on their power clothes, as well. I notice a big splatter of Powderhorn on Rebecca's skirt. Polly has kneeled down in some Chilibean, and it is now all over her stockings and skirt as well. There is a dab of Chilibean on her nose.

But none of them seem to be minding any of this. Tom is having the most fun, chewing on his cigar and singing dirty barroom songs.

"*Bang bang Lulu, Lulu bang bang.*
"*Bang bang Lulu, Lulu bang bang,*" he sings.

The women laugh and the men sing along.

"*Lulu had a boyfriend, her boyfriend had a truck.*
"*Lulu liked to shift the gears,*
"*Her boyfriend liked to. . .*"

Suddenly, the men stop singing.

"*Fuck!*" the women shout.

Everybody in the room laughs. Then, Tom leads them through another stanza and by the end of the song everyone has joined in again.

Painting the White House

"*Fuck!*" the women shout again, only this time louder.

Everyone in the room laughs harder.

I sit on the conference table to watch all this. My legs dangle over the side. I have an apple in my lunch box. I take it out and munch on it while I'm watching this little show. In essence, that's all I can do because they are using all my rollers and brushes. Today's copy of the *Washington Post* is sitting on the conference table. I page through it, occasionally glancing at them to make sure nobody screws up the job.

Anyway, I'm deep into the sports page when I look up and notice Iris standing in the doorway. She has her hands on her hips and appears ready to drop dead. I practice some kinesics and bring my forefinger to my lips and make a motion that I hope Iris will interpret to mean to keep her mouth shut about this. She smiles, nods, and leaves.

Suddenly, I remember the twenty-dollar bill that Tom thrust into my pocket. I smile at my new fortune. I fish into the pocket of my overalls and retrieve the money. I unfold the bill. I have never given it much thought, but it is a fact that the White House is on the back of the twenty-dollar bill. On the front of the bill is Andrew Jackson. Andy and me eye each other. He doesn't seem happy. Actually, he looks downright sour. I wonder what was bugging him on the day he posed for his twenty-dollar bill portrait. I flip over the bill and study the rendering of the White House. Nothing special, you know, just another picture of the White House. The image has been etched in green ink. My guess is the printers at the Bureau of Engraving used Sea Spinach or perhaps Jungle Fever. I make a mental note to check my chips at some point. I shove the money back into my pocket and return to the sports page.

The job was supposed to take three days. Instead, with five people working, it is all wrapped up by three o'clock. They didn't even break for lunch. I did, munching a turkey sandwich right there on the conference room table in the Roosevelt Room of the White House.

* * *

While they are working, I also manage to slip out of the Roosevelt Room for a few minutes. I head down the hall to the Treaty Room, which is another small meeting room. It is going to be my next job. The walls are very dark green, the trim and the ceiling are white. The furniture is Victorian and most of the upholstery as well as the draperies are deep wine. Iris says she thinks there is too much green in the White House and I agree. We decide that a continuation of the wine motif on the walls wouldn't be a bad idea. I pick out some dark colors, such as Crane and Pony Express. Iris leans toward something lighter, and she picks out China Grove and Smokey Lilac. This time, we call in Hazel. She sides with me, and her selection is Pony Express. For the trim, we go with Smokey Lilac. A little concession to Iris from time to time is not a bad idea.

So I dawdle in the Treaty Room, take some measurements and figure out how much paint I'll need. Then, I return to the Roosevelt Room and check on my assistants.

They are doing a good job. Polly and Rebecca have a real talent for it, as does Luis. The others could probably do a decent enough job in their own homes, but they should not think about turning professional.

I'm not going to tell that to them, though. I'm hoping they have their next meeting in the Treaty Room, right at about the time I'm cracking open a gallon of Pony Express.

Soon they are finished. I must admit that I have never seen a happier bunch of White House aides in the many weeks I have been working here.

They even help me clean up.

As he is leaving, Tom tells me that if anybody asks about Warren Adams's attempted suicide, I should keep my mouth shut. I promise him that I will.

He winks, and then he is out the door.

As for me, I'm delighted. The room is done and I can leave early. Good thing, because that means I can run over to Nancy's house today to have sex with my ex-wife.

The Pony Express Room

Nancy tells me she has to put her clothes back on because she must go to the zoo today. She tells me this right after we have sex. She sits up in bed, lights a cigarette and says she has to go look at some monkeys.

"Monkeys?" I ask.

"I'm doing research for a chapter in my book on kinesics. Three students are going to meet me at the zoo and help. Do you want to go along?"

Well, what the hell, I think. I don't have anything to do for the rest of the afternoon—Tom and his crew have taken care of my work—and I haven't been to the zoo since I was a kid, so I dress as well and we drive over to the National Zoo in my truck. We take Connecticut Avenue and park in the lot near Rock Creek behind the reptile house. There, we find three undergraduates waiting for us. Nancy tells them I'm a research associate. I chat with the students for a few minutes while Nancy buys the passes to the zoo. Two are boys, one is a girl. The boys' names are Tad and Ted; the girl's name is Tammy. Tad tells me he's on the football team. I learn that none of the three students are linguistic anthropology majors, but they have taken a class with Professor Dewey to satisfy their elective requirements. All three are having trouble with the course and Professor Dewey has told them they can earn extra credit if they help her with this research project. Tad tells me he's an art history major while Ted says he is majoring in Spanish literature. Tammy says she hasn't declared a major yet, but at the present she is leaning toward international relations. She isn't sure she wants to declare that as a major, though, because she would have to learn a foreign language and she doesn't know whether she wants to make that kind of commitment to her major. I smile and wish them well. To me, they all look like future house painters.

Anyway, their job today is to take notes. Nancy will be leading them around the zoo, giving her impressions of what she sees and they are to write down what she says. They are also to write down their own impressions of what they see. Nancy asks me if I want to take notes as well, but I beg off. I haven't practiced linguistic anthropology in something like twenty years, so I am sure I'm a bit rusty.

The whole idea of going to the zoo, Nancy tells me, is to study how animals perform kinesics. Nancy says it is her theory that animals engage in a high level of kinesics because their verbal skills are so limited. She intends to devote a whole chapter in her book to animal kinesics. Nancy says she is very excited about the project today.

"Animals can grunt at each other, growl at each other and make other glottal sounds, but they just can't stop and talk to each other," Nancy says. I look over at the three students and they are all writing down what she says.

We start at the monkey house, which is near where we have parked. At the first cage, Nancy spots two spider monkeys, lazily hanging upside down by their tails.

They are facing each other.

"Watch carefully," Nancy says in a whisper. "Let's see what they do."

For the longest time, the two monkeys do nothing.

I think they're asleep and I'm about to suggest that we should move on when one of them yawns.

"Look!" Nancy exclaims. "Look what he did! What do you think it means?"

I want to tell her that it probably means the monkey is thinking about taking a nap, but I decide not to interrupt important scientific research. I look around and see Nancy's three students taking notes.

Ted raises his hand. Nancy nods toward him.

"Professor Dewey, if that monkey is trying to communicate with his friend through a yawn, isn't it likely that the friend will also respond with some form of non-verbal communication?"

Painting the White House

"It's certainly possible," Nancy says. "Let's keep watching."

Unfortunately, the monkey's friend doesn't do anything. Then, the first monkey yawns again. Everybody makes note of that.

Ted is standing next to me. I lean over and look at his notepad. It says:

4:40 p.m. Monkey yawns.
4:47 p.m. Monkey yawns again.

Nancy tells the students there has already been significant research done on monkeys who communicate non-verbally. She tells them about the Bluto Project.

I know it well. When I was an undergraduate, I wrote a thirty-page term paper on the Bluto Project. Bluto was a monkey who learned a series of hand signals from a linguist. Just easy stuff, though—nothing complicated, such as how to fly a Mercury space capsule. Bluto learned how to ask for a banana or a drink of water or a toy by making a few simple hand signals. The linguistic anthropology community thought the Bluto Project was the biggest advancement in the understanding of the evolution of language in decades. Would you believe it? All that fuss over a monkey who learned how to ask for a banana by pointing to its mouth. I guess there is a lot I never understood about linguistic anthropology. Maybe it's best I'm a house painter.

I look back at the monkeys hanging upside down by their tails. We are patient, but we see no more non-verbal communication. None of these guys have anything on Bluto.

Finally, we decide to move on. In the next cage we find a couple of chimps. Some little kids are standing in front of the cage, making faces at the chimps. The chimps are making faces back. Everybody's having a good time.

I look over at Nancy and see she's a bit perturbed. "Those kids are just playing and they have the chimps' attention," she says. "The chimps aren't trying to communicate with the kids now, they are just playing. We have to catch the chimps alone, when nobody is distracting them."

Unfortunately, there seem to be kids in front of most of the cages in the monkey house. I guess that's just the way it is with zoos—they attract a lot of kids.

What's a serious linguistic anthropologist to do?

Well, the answer is to move on. We come to Lion and Tiger Hill, and luckily for us there aren't that many kids standing around the fence. We see a lion lounging in the grass. He is rolled over on his back, paws in the air. He looks sleepy. Suddenly, he yawns.

Nancy perks up.

"Did everybody see that!" she exclaims.

The three undergraduates nod their heads and make note of the lion's yawn.

And then he yawns again. Nancy is positively giddy. She grabs my arm and squeezes tight.

And just when I think the old fellow in the grass can't do enough for the cause of linguistic research, he yawns a third time.

Nancy is practically beside herself. She starts talking very quickly, offering her students a loose but rapid-fire train of thoughts and ideas. They take notes vigorously.

"I think this lion is going to yawn a lot...hmmm...but think of how little we saw the monkeys yawn. Do you think predators yawn more than herbivores? Perhaps. Monkeys lead happy and peaceful lives out in the wild, and when they are brought up in captivity they usually lead happy and peaceful lives as well. After all, they have plenty of trees to swing from here, plenty of bananas to eat and plenty of kids to make faces at. But a lion—he's a killer out in the wild. He hunts and stalks and knows the taste of fresh, warm blood. Here, in the zoo, he can do little more than roll around on his back all day. It is true: when he is hungry he is fed, but I'm sure he misses the thrill of the chase, the excitement he finds in stalking his prey, the rush of adrenaline he must feel when he outruns the gazelle or the antelope and makes the kill. And so here in the zoo he yawns. I think he is trying to tell us he is bored."

I didn't know you could say all that with just a yawn, but everybody else is nodding their heads in apparent agreement with Nancy. I look back at the lion. He yawns again. So do I.

We leave the cat hill and I mention that I'm hungry and a hot dog would taste really good right about now. The students are in agreement. Nancy, who wants to continue with her research, launches a protest but finally relents. We buy some hot dogs and coffee from a vendor, and although it is early February and a bit chilly outside today, the late afternoon sun is pleasantly warm so we find a picnic table and go to work on

Painting the White House

our wieners. I slather lots of mustard on mine, but like an idiot I walk away from the vendor without even thinking of relish.

Everybody munches food, but Nancy wants to talk about animal kinesics.

"One of the most fascinating examples of animal kinesics is the honeybee," she says. "Scientists have been studying the bee as far back as 1920 and have come up with some startling conclusions about nonverbal language among animals.

"For example, researchers found that when one bee finds a source of nectar, he'll go back to the hive and return later with other bees. How does he tell them that he's found nectar? What does he say: 'Hey, guys! Follow me...I just found some really tasty mums?'

"Well, research showed the bee does a dance! When he returns to the hive, he shakes his body in such a way to demonstrate not only that he has found nectar, but that he knows where it is and explains to the other bees, in the dance, how to get there. Isn't that incredible?"

Tad and Tammy agree that the dance of the bee is truly incredible. Ted is munching on his hot dog and chooses not to say anything.

Nancy takes another bite on her hot dog. The other students are trying to write down what she says and chew their food at the same time. Some of them find it difficult to keep up. I'm lucky because I don't have to take notes, so I have no problem chewing my food.

"So the bee does this dance," Nancy continues between bites, "and it turns its little body around and around to show the other bees how far the nectar is from the hive. While it's turning its body, it's also doing a waggle—you know, it is sort of shaking its little butt. The further away the nectar, the fewer number of turns. Did everyone hear what I said? The further away the food, the fewer times the bee turned around. But although the number of turns decreases as the distance grows, the number of waggles increases."

"Why?" asks Tammy.

"Nobody knows," Nancy shrugs. "I guess they couldn't ask the bees."

Everyone chews that over for a bit.

"What about direction?" Tad asks. "How do the other bees know which direction to fly toward the nectar?"

"Interesting question," says Nancy. "It has to do with the direction of the waggle. During the dance, if the bee waggles its butt in the direction of the sun, that means the other bees should fly toward the sun to find the nectar. If the waggle is done away from the sun, that means the nectar is opposite the sun."

I finish my hot dog but I'm still hungry, so I waggle my butt over to the vendor and buy another. This time I heap on the relish. I also notice some onions, and I pile those on as well.

When I return to the table, I find Nancy telling the students about the jackdaw. The jackdaw is a big ugly black bird, she says, but is nevertheless a vital player in semantic research.

"Animal kinesics isn't confined to the hunt for food. Many animals do mating dances. The male and female jackdaws do a variety of movements with their body parts to show each other that they are ready to mate. The male spreads his wings before the female, proudly rearing his head and staring into his mate's eyes. The female jackdaw turns her eyes away from the male, but darts instantaneous glances toward him."

"Then what happens?" asks Ted.

"Then they mate," says Nancy.

"Oh," says Ted.

Everybody writes that down.

Nancy continues.

"After they mate, the female performs little dances in the presence of the male. She squats before him, she makes her wings and tail quiver, she lowers her head. Scientists have concluded that there is an enormous amount of semantic value in the movements of the wings and tails of jackdaws."

By now, everyone has finished their hot dogs. It also seems to me that Nancy has run out of things to say about honeybees and jackdaws. She suggests that we move on, and we do.

We spend about another hour at the zoo. On our way out, I ask Tammy if I can see her notepad. Here's what she wrote down:

Monkey: Two yawns.
Lion: Four yawns.
Tiger: Washed fur with tongue.
Ostrich: Pecked at feathers with beak.
Zebra: Flared lips.
Giraffe: Shook head several times.

Painting the White House

Black bear: One yawn.

Alligator: Swished tail. Also snapped jaws open and shut. Professor Dewey says activity is probably not a yawn.

Coyote: Dangled tongue from mouth.

Cockatoo: Fluttered wings. Professor Dewey says this may be significant because cockatoos can mimic verbal speech. More study needed here.

Gorilla: Scratched genitals.

Elephant: One yawn.

* * *

We leave the students in the parking lot. They are excited about taking part in kinesic research today and promise Nancy they'll be available to help her on her book if she needs them again.

I take Nancy back to her place. By now, it is close to six o'clock. She tells me she is absolutely delighted with our work at the zoo today and thinks it would be worth it to return for another walk-through. In the meantime, she'll have the students type up their notes. Nancy says she thinks the chapter on animal kinesics will be one of the best in the book.

"That monkey. . .the way he made his yawn. I think he was definitely attempting to communicate non-verbally. I'd like to go back and just spend hours and hours watching the monkeys. Of course, monkeys make sounds too, you know, but I think they do a lot of their communicating by movements of their bodies. Their yawns could be very significant to semantic research."

Nancy is pacing through the house, talking excitedly about all the possibilities she sees in monkey yawn research.

"Maybe there is even a grant proposal in this," she says. "Do you know what I'd like to do? I'd like to start with about a dozen monkeys, put them in a lab and attach sensors to them. That way, we can document whether yawning is actually a way of communicating non-verbally. We could measure their heart rates, their galvanic skin response, even their erections.

"Of course, that will take a lot of money. Research monkeys are expensive and so is lab time. It may cost $10 million, maybe more. I'm not sure the university has that kind of money."

She talks on and on about animal kinesics for about ten more minutes. I am so bored. I suddenly recall that Jodie Robbins told me she majored in linguistic anthropology at Yale. I try to picture Jodie in Nancy's classroom, debating the theory behind the waggle dance of the bee, and I come up blank. No wonder Jodie flunked out. That girl definitely needs some career counseling.

And then I wonder how I sat through four years of this bullshit as an undergraduate myself. Thinking back, I can't believe I found it interesting at the time. True, I found enough to say about Bluto to fill up thirty pages in a term paper, but two days after graduation I was working on a paint crew for a guy named Blackie and I don't think Blackie, to this day, gives a damn how many times a honeybee waggles its ass. When he hired me, he didn't ask to see my paper on Bluto.

Of course, I had to go to work for Blackie because I wasn't accepted into graduate school. What if I had? Well, I would probably have been at the zoo today, showing a bunch of students how monkeys yawn and alligators swish their tales and expecting my students to write down everything I say so that they, too, can get into graduate school. And then what would happen? Twenty years from now, they'll be showing their students around the zoo speculating on the possible semantic meaning of a monkey's yawn.

I think I'll stick to painting houses. It doesn't help the cause of science, but it sure makes the room look nice.

Anyway, I listen to Nancy drone on about animal kinesics and then, finally, I decide to show her some animal kinesics of my own. I put my arms around her.

"What time does Franklin usually get home?" I ask.

"Late," she says.

"Terrific," I tell her, and then I take Nancy back to bed, where she makes lots of little monkey sounds.

* * *

When I arrive home, I dive right into bed and fall asleep very quickly. It's been a long day. First, I had to supervise the painting crew in the Roosevelt Room, then I had to walk around the zoo for a couple of hours and in the meantime I had to satisfy the sexual desires of a forty-year-old linguistic anthropology professor while listening to her babble on about why jackdaws spread their wings and monkeys yawn at each other.

I laugh at all I have done today.

And then I decide not to buy Nancy's book.

Painting the White House
* * *

I start off fresh the next morning. I leave my apartment early because I have to stop at the paint store, where I ask them to make up a few gallons of Pony Express and Smokey Lilac. By eight o'clock in the morning I'm in the Treaty Room and the job is going well. Tom Thatcher comes by.

"Want to help?" I ask.

Tom smiles and picks up a paint brush. He dabs it in some Smokey Lilac, kneels down and goes to work on the baseboard. I notice Tom has become especially good at cutting in, which makes me proud. I think I understand now the rush Nancy must feel when she talks to her students about what makes monkeys yawn.

But he has other troubles—his brush work, for example. He sort of pokes the brush on the woodwork and that leaves splotches. It is a bad habit and I have no idea where he may have picked it up. Certainly, not from me.

Finally, I can take no more. I pick up another brush.

"Watch me and listen to what I have to say," I tell him.

I show him how to dip the brush into the paint. "You wet the brush about half-way up the bristles, then you tap it against the side of the can. That removes the excess paint, but it still gets your brush good and wet. Hold the brush at an angle and push the paint...like this..."

I show him how to push the paint.

"You don't want to dab it on or slap it on...push it on."

He watches me carefully. Then, he wets his brush and tries it. He is doing much better. He is having a good time, but I can tell something is pressing on his mind. I let him work, though. Sometimes, painting will help you work out your problems. It is good exercise for the mind. A lot of painters I know will bring a boom box to the job, turn it up high and let it blast away all day. Not me. I work in silence. I want no distractions. I want to give my mind the opportunity to work on something other than painting.

I can tell that Tom is working something over in his mind. His kinesics tell me so.

"You know," he says after a while, "I didn't come here to help you paint the baseboard."

He stands up, returns the paint brush to the can and wipes his hands on a rag. "Some reporters have been asking around about Warren Adams," Tom says. "A couple of them have said they heard that a house painter may know something about what happened. Please. . .if you know something, keep your mouth shut? OK?"

"OK," I tell him.

Tom smiles. He trusts me. We have applied a lot of interior flat latex together and there is a bond between us now.

"Thanks," he says.

I think, somehow, learning how to paint a room has taken a bit of the edge off Tom. I don't see him as the take-no-prisoners guy he was before he learned how to work a paint roller. Paint will do that for you, I believe. Working with your hands. . .accomplishing something of value. . .making the world look nicer through a new paint job. . .it all means something, and I think Tom's psyche is now tuned in to it. I think Tom is a better person for it, and since Tom Thatcher has a lot to say about the federal government and the quality of life in America, I think the United States will be a better place to live now that Tom and his aides have learned how to apply latex wall paint. Call me a patriotic fool, but I really believe that.

Tom turns to leave, but pauses. "When are you going to do our offices? Why don't you sit down with Polly and go over some ideas about color? If you have a minute, would you bring your samples around?"

I tell him I would be delighted, and he leaves.

I finish the Treaty Room later that week. The Pony Express looks pretty good in there.

* * *

The Lincoln Sitting Room is next. It is a small room on the southeast corner of the second floor. Over the years, members of the White House staff used it as an office, but in recent years it was set aside as a place where the president could have a private chat with a dignitary, a visitor or whomever.

The walls are done in a beige fabric and Janey has told Iris she wants to keep the fabric on the walls because it goes well with the burnt orange carpet and upholstery on the Victorian furniture. The trim needs to be redone, though. There is wainscoting and a chair rail, large pilaster-headed columns framing the draperies and crown molding along the ceiling. The window casings are very ornate. All the trim is painted white.

Painting the White House

We decide the trim looks fine in white. We sift through the samples, and it doesn't take long before we select Cirrus Whisper.

Cirrus Whisper is a very white white. That's as best as I can describe it. A very white white.

Personally, I'm relieved that I only have to do the trim in the Lincoln Sitting Room. I look over the job and decide it will probably take me a day or two to finish the room.

That's good, because I am soon to learn that my time will be in great demand by the mass media.

The Cirrus Whisper Room

When Warren Adams walked out of the Yellow Oval Room with a nasty welt around his neck, only about a few dozen people noticed it. He was, after all, one hell of a mess that day, as you may recall.

The chief of staff to the president can't exactly walk down the hall of the White House looking like shit without people mentioning it to one another. And since there are a couple hundred people who work in the White House, things do tend to get noticed. It doesn't take long for the insiders to conclude that he may have tried to kill himself. Some good detective work leads a number of White House snoops to my trail. One of them is, of course, Tom Thatcher, who has already advised me to keep my mouth shut.

Another is Iris, who also advises me not to talk about Warren.

"Let the president take care of this matter," she says.

I tell her I will.

A third person who sniffs out the story is a guy named Edward M. Carter.

He works for the *New York Times*.

* * *

Before I tell you what happens next, you have to understand something about reporters. Most of them don't know anything about the news they cover. Their editors move them around so much that they hardly ever develop any expertise in one particular field. It's as if Nancy would spend years studying and teaching linguistic anthropology and

Painting the White House

then suddenly the president of her university decides she should teach drama. She won't study it, she won't go to school to learn it, she will just start acting as though she knows everything there is to know about the theater. Pretty silly, eh? Newspapers, TV networks, and political websites don't think so. As a result, the news you read in the paper or see on TV or online is usually written by people who have no business writing it. They are simply unqualified to write about foreign affairs, domestic policy, the economy, social issues, the theater or whatever.

But newspapers, TV networks and websites just can't go out and hire an economist to write the economic news. Most economists want too much money and, besides, hardly any of them know how to write or possess the skills of an expert enunciator as they stare back into a TV camera. So the news organizations are stuck with hiring journalists who work cheap and are good writers or, at least, they know how to write well enough to fool their readers into thinking they know what they are writing about. Or, if they work for a TV network, they are very good at pronunciation.

And so when Eddie Carter saw his lifelong dream fulfilled—to be assigned to the White House beat by the most influential newspaper in the world—he was determined that from the outset, no one would ever guess that he didn't know anything about the White House or how it worked.

One might even argue that Eddie knows as much about the White House as I do. After all, we both started working here on the same day.

Of course, I started in the Lincoln Bedroom applying a satiny coat of Buffalo Bill to the walls. Eddie started in the press room, where he sat in the assigned seat of the *New York Times* for his first press briefing. I've been in the press room. It is in the West Wing and has cobalt blue walls. Anyway, you may recall that on that first day, I heard the story of Jodie Robbins' life while she was clad in a very revealing Japanese kimono. At about the same time Jodie was chain-smoking and telling me about her short but tortured existence, Eddie Carter was receiving a briefing on how the Robbins administration intends to respond to the Senate's rejection of a bill to declare the Rocky Mountain Spotted White Sparrow an endangered species.

Between you and me, I think I had the better day.

But don't mention that to Eddie. Right after the briefing, Eddie returned to his newspaper's Washington bureau, where he banged out fourteen inches of copy on whether the administration would stick by its commitment to protect the Rocky Mountain Spotted White Sparrow. The *Times* ran the story on the same page as the obituaries. Since there are very few Rocky Mountain Spotted White Sparrows in midtown Manhattan, it is questionable as to how many people actually read the story within the primary circulation area of the *New York Times*. Still, Eddie had his first bylined article from the White House.

(Let me pause here to add that none of the major TV networks as well as none of the cable news networks carried the story on their broadcasts that night. Most of the Internet skipped the story as well, although it is my understanding the Facebook page for the United Birdwatchers of the United States of America was dominated by chatter focusing on the fate of the Rocky Mountain Spotted White Sparrow.)

Actually, I think Eddie should be congratulated for coming as far as he did with so little talent. Eddie's father owns a small newspaper in upstate Pennsylvania and he sent Eddie off to the University of Pennsylvania with the idea that he would return after graduation and eventually become editor. But Eddie had other ideas. After going to school in a city the size of Philadelphia, Eddie knew he could never return to a tiny coal town. So after graduation, he landed a job at the *Philadelphia Daily News*, where he churned out bland but important stories about city government.

Eddie always did have a problem with writing. He was simply just never very good at it. The copy desk had to fix up his work every night. A lot of journalists complain about copy editors who change their work. Not Eddie. He knew he couldn't write and he really appreciated it when his work was improved by his editors. (Eddie had a particular problem with knowing the difference between "who" and "whom." He was also notorious for mixing up "their" and "they're" and "it's" and "its.")

Eddie was determined to eventually work for the *New York Times*. He knew, of course, that when he applied for a position at the *Times* the editors would see only his finished bylined clips that he submitted with his resume; indeed, they would never know the work others had put into fixing up his stories. He was sure there were plenty of people at the *Times* who were as lousy as he was when it came to writing, so he wasn't worried about not fitting in.

Still, the first time he applied he was rejected. Eddie resolved to try again. He hunkered back down to work at the *Daily News*, determined to make an impression.

It didn't take long.

Although Eddie was a bit of a failure when it came to the writing part, he was, nevertheless, a good reporter when it came to the snooping part. Soon, Eddie latched onto a good tip about a city bond fraud. He wrote a series on the fraud, exposed some graft and was a runner-up for the Pulitzer Prize. That made an impression. Soon, he was granted a second interview at the *Times*, and he had his job.

Eddie spent a year in a suburban bureau in Westchester, New York, then a year covering the New Jersey State House in Trenton. Eddie proved to be quite deft at office politics, and eventually had himself transferred to the New York State House in Albany. He wrote good newsy stories that made it onto the front page of the *Times*. A lot of his stories were picked up by Internet sites and republished. His name became very familiar among New Yorkers.

Of course, most of his stories lacked complete sentence structure as well as the elements of good grammar, but the copy desk took care of him. Eddie never complained when the copy editors changed his stories and, as such, he had few enemies at the newspaper. When a job opened in the Washington bureau, Eddie put in for it and held his breath. Now, Washington bureau jobs at the *New York Times* aren't given out without a great deal of thought and deliberation by the editors. Finally, the choice came down to Eddie and another reporter. The other reporter considered himself the reincarnation of Ernest Hemingway and was known to really bitch and moan when the night desk changed his copy. Eddie didn't have that reputation and, as a result, he had a lot of friends among the senior editors—all of whom had spent time on the copy desk. It turned out to be no contest, after all. Eddie won the job in Washington and Hemingway went back to covering the public transportation beat on Long Island.

For Eddie, winning a place in the Washington bureau was half the job. He still had a way to go before he could move up to the White House beat, which was his eventual goal. Eddie started out covering the minor bureaucracy—reporting on the activities in the Commerce and Agriculture departments and similar "below the fold" agencies. But turnover in the *Times* Washington bureau is surprisingly high. In his first two years in the bureau, Eddie saw some of his colleagues take buyouts, due largely to the dwindling fortunes of the print industry. Others left for websites, such as the Daily Beast and HuffPost. A couple of reporters took jobs in the Robbins administration as press attaches. One fellow left the bureau to write a book. As all this was going on, Eddie kept moving up.

Finally, the White House job opened up. Eddie, who still steadfastly refused to complain about copy editors, applied for the opening. He found just as many friends among the senior editors in New York as he always had. In his four years in Washington, his stories had been remarkably bland, his writing mostly unimproved and his knowledge of punctuation still lacking.

The job was his.

And three weeks after attending his first briefing on the administration's Rocky Mountain Spotted White Sparrow assistance policy, a maintenance man told Eddie that Warren Adams tried to kill himself in the White House, and that a house painter had talked him out of it.

* * *

The Lincoln Sitting Room doesn't take long to paint at all. As you know, I am only supposed to re-do the trim. I start early in the morning and by mid-afternoon I decide to wrap up for the day. I've finished the wainscotting and the crown molding, but I still have to do the fireplace, the window casings and the baseboard. I decide I can finish that work quickly tomorrow and perhaps I can even start on the next room. For now, though, I am finished for the day. I decide to run home, take a quick shower and give Nancy a call. Maybe Franklin is working late again.

I am loading up my truck in front of the North Portico when a skinny little guy with a cigarette poking out of his mouth approaches me. He is dressed well in an expensive suit and silk necktie that has maroon and gray diagonal stripes. He has on a long black overcoat, but he leaves it unbuttoned. His hair is very neat and trimmed just right, and it's my guess he wears a toupee. He tells me he is Edward M. Carter, White House correspondent for the *New York Times*, and he wants to know whether I'm the guy who has been painting the rooms in the White House.

I nod.

Painting the White House

He smiles. "Mind if we chat for a few minutes?"

I have a feeling I know what he wants to chat about. Warren, of course. I have been warned by Tom and Iris that reporters have been asking about me. They have both advised me to keep my mouth shut. What am I to do? If I say I don't want to talk, Eddie will know why and that will make him even more curious. I glance at him. He has Sunset Sea eyes—sort of greenish blue, if you check the chips. They are very warm, and he has a way of cocking his eyebrows and furrowing his forehead that makes me think he isn't so dangerous, after all. I must remember to mention this to Nancy, because I think it will help in her kinesics research. I decide that it won't do any harm to talk to him, but I make a mental note to mostly listen and let him do the talking.

So I say, "I don't mind if we talk, not at all. What do you want to talk about?"

Here is where Eddie shows his stuff. A lesser reporter would blurt out: *What do you know about the attempted suicide of Warren Adams?* Not Eddie. He takes a drag on his cigarette and lets the blue smoke slowly escape through his nose while he purses his lips together. He looks very serious. I really must mention this guy to Nancy; he is a master of kinesics. Perhaps, she will want to interview him for her book.

Finally, he says, "I guess you've painted a lot of rooms in the White House by now."

I nod.

"What were some of the rooms you painted?"

I tell him I painted the Lincoln Bedroom, the Blue Room, the Red Room, the Yellow Oval Room and a bunch of other rooms. He pulls out a little notepad and takes a lot of notes.

"Have you painted any offices?"

"I don't think so, not yet at least."

"No offices at all?"

"Nope."

He looks disappointed. Then, I remember what Tom Thatcher has told me and snap my fingers. His eyes brighten. "What is it?" he says.

"Somebody who works for Tom Thatcher. . .I think her name is Polly. . I'm meeting with her soon to go over some paint samples. Tom wants me to paint his staff's offices. So I haven't painted any offices yet, but I plan to do some soon. Does that help?"

He writes down everything I tell him, but I can tell by the look on his face that I'm not giving him what he had been expecting.

"You sure you haven't painted any offices?" he asks. "Maybe you painted Warren Adams' office?"

I shake my head. I am absolutely being truthful with him. I try to make my facial expression convey this message to him, but I guess I have not mastered kinesics quite so well as he has.

"Are we finished?" I ask.

He scratches his chin and glances away from me. He kicks the pavement with the toe of his shoe. Then, he thrusts his left hand into his suit pocket.

This guy's talent for kinesics is absolutely out of the world.

"Maybe one or two more questions," he says.

"Shoot."

"Have you met Warren while you've been working here?"

I nod.

"Did any of his behavior seem strange to you?"

I shrug my shoulders and wonder if Eddie guesses something. You know, I never was a very good liar. I hope my kinesics have not given me away.

"A lot of people have told me that Warren's behavior has been strange of late," Eddie says. "Some people have told me he tried to kill himself in his office by slashing his wrists with a razor blade, and that you walked in on him and stopped him from doing it."

"How did I do that?"

"The way I heard it, you showed up to paint his office one morning and he was in there, working on his wrists with a razor blade. You tackled him. . .knocked him right on his ass. . .and were able to stop the bleeding by tying a tourniquet with some rags you had with you. You're a hero, you know that? Instead of keeping your mouth shut about it, you should tell people what really happened. And besides, if Warren is that unstable he shouldn't have such an important job in the White House, for Christ's sake. Maybe the best thing for him is for a story to come out about what really happened in his office. That way, he can resign and seek some professional psychiatric help."

Eddie drops his cigarette to the pavement, crushes it with his toe and lights another cigarette. He draws in a large gust of smoke, and savors it

Painting the White House

as it fills his lungs. He releases the smoke slowly, and it drifts away from us in the cold gusty February breeze.

Finally, he says, "Come on, why don't you tell me what really happened in his office that morning?"

I shrug.

"Listen," I tell him. "I'm going to tell you something because I want the truth told, but I don't want you to use my name. I'm only a house painter, you know, so you should really get the story from somebody who has an important position in the White House. But I will tell you this: Warren Adams is a decent individual. He has some troubles; we all have troubles. I found Warren Adams alone one morning and he was trying to solve his troubles the best way he knew how. He needed somebody to talk to and I gave him a pretty good ear. I think he'll be OK. That's all I have to say."

Eddie takes notes feverishly while I am speaking. He glances at me while his pen is moving.

When I finish, he says, "You are saying then, that he did try to kill himself and you talked him out of it?"

"I said all I'm going to say about it."

"Can I use your name?"

"No. Don't even say the house painter told you this, OK?"

He smiles.

"OK. What happened to the razor blade? Do you still have it?"

"I'm not saying anything more," I tell him. I return to loading the truck. He thanks me and walks away. I go home, take a shower and call Nancy's phone number. Franklin answers, so I hang up. That night, I eat at MacDonald's. Then I go to bed early.

The next morning, I arrive early at the White House, head for the Lincoln Sitting Room and start on the fireplace. The work is going quickly when I notice Iris in the doorway.

"Have you seen the *New York Times* this morning?"

I am not in the habit of reading the *New York Times*, so I tell her no, I haven't.

She has a copy of the newspaper folded under her arm. She shows me the front page. In the upper left hand corner, above the fold on Page One, is this story:

Hal Marcovitz

White House Chief of Staff Adams
Attempted to Kill Self, Sources Say
By Edward M. Carter

WASHINGTON—White House Chief of Staff Warren Adams tried to take his own life by slashing his wrists with a razor blade, sources high in the Robbins administration have confirmed.

The attempted suicide reportedly occurred early in January in his office in the West Wing of the White House. Sources in the administration say President Robbins has had no knowledge of his chief aide's suicide attempt.

"Warren Adams is a decent individual; he has troubles, we all have troubles," said the source who confirmed the story. The source holds a position of influence in the Robbins White House and has asked to remain anonymous.

Congressional leaders said they were shocked to learn of Mr. Adams' apparent mental problems. Most of them served alongside Mr. Adams in the House of Representatives when he was a congressman from Rhode Island.

"I hope Warren gets the help he needs," said House Speaker Richard M. Wilson.

Leaders in the Senate were likewise concerned...

The story jumps to the inside. It goes on to say that White House spokesmen were unavailable for comment, but congressional leaders were speculating that the president would have no choice now but to fire Warren.

"Did this guy Carter talk to you?" Iris asks.

"He stopped me yesterday and asked a few questions, but I told him nothing."

I am wondering, though, whether I am much better at kinesics than I realize, and that somehow I managed to confirm Warren's attempted suicide by making body motions. I decide that I will have to take up this matter with Nancy.

"Really," I say, "he asked me some questions about Warren and I told him I couldn't help."

I glance at Iris as I am telling her all this. She looks skeptical. I can tell that the finger of guilt is pointing at me.

Painting the White House

"Honestly," I say, at last. "Do I look like a person who holds a position of influence in the Robbins White House? Hey! I'm the house painter."

Iris laughs and that makes her girth shake. She is wearing a red and black number today with a hemline that ends well above the knee. I'm wondering whatever possessed Iris, who is half the size of an SUV, to want to show off her legs.

"Everybody else is going to want this story now," she says. "All the other newspapers will have to print their versions of the story, the networks are going to want to do their sound bites and I'm sure the tabloid TV shows will come snooping around. And I don't even want to think of what's going to end up on Twitter."

"Do you think they'll want to talk to me?" I ask.

Iris shakes her head.

"Why would they want to interview you? You're only the house painter."

* * *

All three networks lead their newscasts that night with the story of Warren's attempted suicide. CNN runs reports on it all day. Fox News analysts predict that the Robbins Administration will commit political suicide if the president doesn't fire Warren. Yes, that was actually the speculation over at Fox News. Political suicide. Some of the commentators on MSNBC whine as well, but they invariably end their soliloquies with friendly, knowing smiles. Reporters on National Public Radio provide their typically vapid stories on the affair—mostly with information lifted from Eddie's story in the *Times*. Social media provides its own variations on the story, some of it fueled by Russian bots. The next morning, all the major daily newspapers with White House correspondents publish their reports on the attempted suicide of Warren Adams.

And nobody gets it right. Everybody basically repeats what Eddie wrote the day before: that Warren tried to kill himself by slashing his wrists in his office. Nobody reports that the president's chief of staff did not attempt to slash his wrists but, rather, tried to end his own life through self-ligature. Or that the incident occurred in the Yellow Oval Room, not in his office. Or, that the White House painter caught him in the act and saved his life. Naturally, I am a bit put out, but I know enough to keep my mouth shut. And Iris is right, you know. Nobody asks to interview me because, after all, I am the house painter.

Mostly, they interview Tom. He is quoted in all the major newspaper stories and on the networks, and I must say he acquits himself well. Tom is, indeed, an eloquent spokesperson for the administration. Warren refuses to make himself available for interviews, which I can understand. The president has no comment.

While all this is going on around me I manage to finish the Lincoln Sitting Room. Cirrus Whisper was a good choice all along. It adds a new luster to the woodwork in the room and Janey was right in deciding to leave the burnt-orange motif as is.

Anyway, I finish cleaning up when I suddenly recall that Polly down in Tom's office wants to see some samples. I gather up my chips and head to the West Wing.

The Wild Napa Grape Room

Tom's suite of offices is surprisingly quiet. I guess that's because Tom hasn't been in all day, what with all the shuttling back and forth among TV news bureaus he has had to do. The story in the *New York Times* has sent shock waves throughout the White House, and damage control has apparently fallen into Tom's lap.

Back in Tom's suite of offices, though, it appears nothing more than another sleepy day in the West Wing.

The sign above the door says "Office of Policy and Planning." I enter and find a circular setup, with a group of desks pushed together in the middle of the room, surrounded by a half-dozen doors leading into small offices. Obviously, Tom and his aides work in the offices while the clerical help sits in the middle. I guess this is the model of the modern American office. Everything seems to be super-efficient.

I notice Luis by the coffee machine in the outer office and I smile, and he gives me a big wave in return. I tell the receptionist I'm the painter and I'm here to see Polly. She punches some buttons on the telephone and whispers something, then she hangs up, points to Polly's office and tells me to go right on in.

I find Polly sitting behind her desk. It is stacked high with typed documents, photocopied pages, that sort of thing. The walls and ceiling in Polly's office are painted off-white—sort of a bland Tuscan Beach. Even the baseboard and the door are Tuscan Beach. I survey the furnishings. You won't find any Duncan Phyfe furniture in here. Polly's office is unlike anything else I have seen in the White House. Everything in here is here for a purpose. Every other room I've painted so far is decorated to impress somebody—tourists, foreign ambassadors, congressional leaders, whomever. Not Polly's office. She has a desk, two chairs, a filing cabinet, a telephone and a computer terminal, all crammed within about a hundred square feet. There is virtually no color in this office. No prints on the walls, no photographs on her desk, no potted plants in the corner, no life at all in here. Everything is very. . . what?. . .functional?

There are no windows. Above us, the light is provided by a recessed fluorescent lighting fixture, its ballast humming like a baritone honeybee. The glow is sickening as well—the twin bulbs projecting an off-yellow Banana Garden, in my estimation. I find it unnerving. The air circulates through louvered heat vents near the ceiling.

My eye catches another drab rectangle of color in the room. It is emanating from the cathode ray tube on her desk. The screen is dark green, very close to a Black Olive I would say. On this field of green are lighter specks of green—characters in a screen of copy. I would describe the characters as an Ocean Kelp, I think. I shudder. If I had to work in this room all day, I think I would go slowly mad.

Polly stands and extends her hand across her desk. She is blonde, about 5-7, although I'm sure she is shorter in her stocking feet. Her hair is tied tightly behind her head. I have noticed that every woman in the White House, for no apparent reason, ties their hair in tight buns behind their heads.

Polly is wearing a white blouse and a skinny black woman's necktie. Her gray wool suit jacket is thrown across a chair on the other side of the room, where I am sure it is picking up some wrinkles. Her skirt is gray wool as well. She wears very thick glasses, very little make-up and very little jewelry.

"Tom told me to pick out some colors for the office," she says. "I guess he figured with my background, I would do the best job."

"Your background?"

"Well, before I changed majors at Princeton, I was a fine arts major."

"Fine arts? Really? You mean you were an artist?"

She nods.

"You painted? I thought you handled a brush a bit better than the others—you did look like a natural."

Painting the White House

Polly laughs.

"Back in college I did some painting—mostly oils and acrylics. I even won a few awards in some campus art shows. But when I started my senior year it occurred to me that I was going to graduate and I probably wasn't going to be able to earn a living selling my paintings. I saw myself with a fine arts degree from Princeton and a job working as a cocktail waitress in an Atlantic City casino. So I changed majors. I had taken a lot of political science courses—artists are very political, you know. By doubling up on some courses in my senior year, I was able to graduate with a degree in liberal arts. My grades were good and I was accepted into graduate school, which is where I was teaching and studying when Tom called. Now, three years later, here I am. Working in the White House."

Funny, but Polly and I had taken similar routes to the White House. She majored in fine arts, but realized before it was too late that she was on a futile course in life. She was able to switch directions before ending up as a cocktail waitress at the Jersey shore. I studied linguistic anthropology, but realized too late that I had made a mistake and ended up working for Blackie.

We talk about this some more. I tell her about my background in linguistic anthropology and my days at George Washington. She is a good listener. She tells me about her years learning how to draw, paint, work with clay, work with silk-screens, and so on.

"One of the reasons I came to work in the White House is because of the art collection—there is a really fabulous art collection here. I don't have much time to spend looking at art, but whenever I'm on my way from one place to another, sometimes I slow down and steal a few minutes in front of a painting."

I tell her that I really don't know much about art, but I have, of course, noticed many fine paintings hanging on the walls of the White House. After all, I have been taking them off the walls so I can paint behind them.

Polly leans forward and lowers her voice, as though she doesn't want anyone to hear what she's about to say. I wonder if the place is bugged.

"Janey doesn't know anything about art," she says. "When the Robbinses moved in, Janey moved all the art work around but she put everything in the wrong places. Do you know she hung Whistler's Nocturne in the Vermeil Room? There is no wall in that room that gets enough light and Nocturne is definitely a painting that needs to be bathed in light."

She shakes her head as she tells me this.

"Jodie has a better taste in art than Janey. Right after Jodie moved in, she made the ushers take her to the basement where the White House art collection is stored. Do you know there are more than three hundred paintings down there? Jodie picked out three or four paintings and had the ushers take them upstairs to her room."

None of that surprises me, of course. Jodie has, after all, told me all about her interest in art. Perhaps, I think, there is a human being inside Jodie screaming to escape, after all.

We talk about art for a long time and then Polly glances at her watch. "Look at the time!" she shrieks.

It is just past six. The clerical help in the outer office has left for the day, but I am sure that Luis, Sam and the others are still hard at work. It is well known around the White House that Tom works his people late every night—sometimes until nine or ten o'clock, or later.

"Hungry?" I ask.

Polly nods and says she can go for a pizza. "Sounds good to me," I say. "I'll bring my paint samples along and we can look at them over dinner."

Polly agrees. "First, let me tell the others I'm leaving," she says.

She picks up her phone and types a text.

The screen says:

Am going out for pizza. Be back soon. Polly.

She looks over the message, then hits send. "OK," she says. "I told everyone what I'm doing. Let's get some pizza."

I'm a bit astonished.

"Did you just text everybody you were leaving for pizza?"

"That's right."

"Why didn't you just shout it out as we were leaving? Everybody's office doors are within ten feet of each other; I'm sure they all would have heard you."

Polly puts on her gray jacket and grabs her purse. "It's much easier to text everyone. Let's go."

I wonder whether Nancy has thought about the effects of texting on language for her book on kinesics. It's pretty tough to communicate with your body parts through a text message, don't you think?

* * *

Polly drives. She owns a cream-colored BMW which she is permitted to park in the White House parking lot. That is a mark of importance around the Executive Mansion. She accelerates onto Pennsylvania Avenue and as she is telling me about a pizza shop she knows in Foggy Bottom, she changes her mind about pizza and decides she would rather have a drink instead. So she takes me to a hip bar on 18th Street in Adams-Morgan named Pinkie's. Polly says she lives in one of the cavernous red brick apartment buildings nearby on Columbia Avenue. When we enter the neighborhood, Polly points out some Adams-Morgan sites to me: where Dwight and Mamie Eisenhower lived while he was a young Army officer, where Admiral Peary lived, where Al Jolson's parents lived, where Lyndon and Lady Bird Johnson lived when he was in the Senate.

Polly finds a parking place. It is cold, so we run briskly to Pinkie's. Her face becomes flushed in the winter air. Winters here in Washington can be biting, and I'm not sure Polly is accustomed to them yet.

Pinkie's is crowded, smoky, noisy. We find ourselves surrounded by an eclectic mix of graduate students, bureaucrats, congressional aides, junior lobbyists and other denizens of the District. Ages range from millennials to Gen Xers to baby boomers. As for me, I'm feeling a bit out of place in this crowd. This is not the type of bar I tend to hang out in, but I decide Polly could probably use a drink to unwind and I am certainly not going to ruin her day by complaining. Still, I am uncomfortable. I let myself eavesdrop on a number of conversations around me and I hear people complaining about their jobs and talking about how rotten it is working for the federal government. I laugh at it all. Truth is, everybody sitting at this bar with Polly and me wants somebody else's job or, perhaps, somebody else's sex life.

Well, not quite everybody. I have the distinct impression that Polly doesn't want anybody else's job, particularly her own. I'm not sure about the sex part, though.

Polly orders a gin and tonic. I order a bloody mary. She takes out a vaping pod and lights up. I munch on a buffalo wing. I'm very hungry.

"You know," she says. "I really enjoy my job. For your first job out of college, working in the White House isn't bad. Don't you think?"

Normally, I would tell her that I agree with her. After all, my first job out of college was as a member of Blackie's crew, and the main benefit I garnered from that experience was learning how to water down paint. Twenty years ago, if somebody had offered me a choice between working for Blackie and working for Tom Thatcher in the White House, I guess I would have to say that I would take the White House.

But I don't think Polly has asked my opinion because she wants me to agree with her. I think she wants me to tell her that she was wrong, that she should never have given up oil painting for a power job in the most powerful building on Earth, that instead of working on speeches and position papers and policy analyses for a fat slob from Florida until nine or ten o'clock every night, she should instead be painting nudes in a Soho brownstone.

I guess I want to tell her this, but I don't because I don't know her well enough. So I say, "I'm sure you're happy," but I say it with a generous amount of kinesics so that I think she catches on to my intended message, which is, "I'm sorry you're not happy."

She draws heavily on her e-cigarette. Then, she sips her gin and tonic. I slurp my bloody mary and munch on another buffalo wing. Something tells me that this will be my dinner.

"I realized four weeks after I went to work for Tom that I had made a terrible mistake. I thought working in the White House would be terrific, challenging, fun, interesting. . .you know, everything every job should be. But it's none of that. Most of the issues we tackle are boring. The hours are long. Tom can be a lout and he usually is. He takes most of the credit when things go well and none of the blame when things go wrong. He isn't nice to us, he never remembers our birthdays and he is constantly trying to pit us against each other.

"And I do miss drawing and painting and working with colors. When Tom told me that he wanted our offices repainted and that you would be around to show me some samples, I became positively excited about it. Know why? It would be my first opportunity in years to do something artistic, something creative. Even if it is just picking out a color for wall paint, I knew it would be an opportunity to use my artistic talent. For one brief moment, I would be an artist again. Isn't that pathetic?"

She reignites her pod.

"When I went to work in the White House I thought I would see the president. . .talk to him. . .tell him what I thought on certain issues. . .exchange ideas with him. . .that sort of thing. Do you know I've worked in the White House for nearly three years and the only place I've ever seen the president is on TV?"

Polly finishes her drink, flags down the bartender and orders another. I am a bit worried that she is talking too loudly, that somebody will overhear and report her problems to some obscure congressman who is looking to make his reputation by climbing all over Abe Robbins' back. Washington can be a cruel town.

I glance from side to side as Polly is talking, and I decide I have nothing to fear. Nobody seems to be paying attention to us. Just as I thought. Self-centered yuppie bastards, every one of them.

She continues.

"I guess if I had gone to work for some big corporation I would be making the same complaints. Maybe I shouldn't be working in an office—I think that may be the problem." She sits up straight on her bar stool and then gazes down at herself. "I don't like wearing the clothes I have to wear. I don't like working for anybody and taking their orders. I don't like giving up my free time to come in on weekends. Do you know I haven't had sex since I left New Jersey? I miss that. Do you know what my apartment looks like? I have a bed and a sofa and a TV and hardly any other furniture. I've been living in Washington for three fucking years and I haven't had a chance to buy any furniture other than a bed and a sofa and a TV. I haven't had to clean the place in weeks because I'm never there long enough to make a mess. Do you know what my last electric bill was? It was thirteen dollars. Thirteen dollars! My electric bill is so low because I never have the chance to turn on my lights or run my appliances."

"If it's so bad, why do you stay?"

Polly shrugs. "I talked to Tom about quitting. It was just a few months ago. He talked me into staying until the end of Abe's first term. Tom can be very sweet when he wants to be. He also throws the patriotic bullshit at you. . .you know, serving your country and your president. I just couldn't say no to him.

"Also, the money isn't bad. It's far more than I could make doing just about anything else. It's tough to walk away from $150,000 a year."

Sure is, I tell her.

"But you were ready to walk away," I quickly add. "At one time, you were ready to tell Tom to shove it. Why didn't you go through with it?"

"I don't know. I guess I realized that I could never go back to. . ."

"To what?"

She gives me a half-smile.

"To painting."

Polly stares down at her drink. She shakes her glass, so that the few drops of colorless gin splash over the few remaining colorless ice cubes. I look down at my own glass. Plenty of rich, red bloody mary left. I drink.

Polly orders another drink, her third. I think we should pick out some colors for the office before she gets too drunk. I lay out some paint chips on the bar. I had selected some bland, off-white colors not unlike the Tuscan Beach that is already on the walls. Polly scowls at them.

"Don't you have anything a bit more colorful?"

"What do you have in mind?"

She says nothing for several minutes. She sits up on her barstool, leaning on her elbows, staring at her reflection in the mirror behind the bar. Noisy motion swirls in back of her, as people dart back and forth, drinks and cigarettes in their hands, a blue cloud of smoke rising above them. In front of her, two busy bartenders dash up and down the bar, frantically mixing drinks in a chaotic yet organized choreography designed so that they can mix drinks and serve customers without slamming into each other. I glance at Polly. This is an important time for her. Lord, how I would love to mind-meld with her now, to hear the voices inside her head unscramble the thoughts of this repressed artist held captive in a world of White House white.

Finally, I say, "Polly, what type of colors would you like to see?"

"Show me something radioactive," she says.

* * *

We leave Pinkie's. I drive, because I think Polly is drunk. Not dead drunk, but tipsy enough to fail a breath test should the DC cops stop our car. I know a paint store that is open late and we head right there. Polly waits in the car. I give the clerk my order, and he starts bitching to me because it's a lot to mix and he wants to close up. He's a tall, red-headed kid with a million freckles and a nasty cold sore on his upper lip. I give him twenty dollars and he shuts up and mixes the paint.

Painting the White House

I frown to myself after I realize what I have just done. The twenty-dollar bill I have just used to bribe the paint store clerk is the same twenty-dollar bill that Tom Thatcher gave me back in the Roosevelt Room. I shrug. Maybe Andrew Jackson will be happier in that kid's pocket than he was in mine. In fact, now that he's out of the White House, Andrew Jackson is probably beside himself with glee.

Back to the job at hand.

I ask for every color to be poured into a quart container. I buy some fresh brushes. Polly has told me to buy some small ones, so I pick out a few half-inch brushes as well as some one-inch brushes. It takes nearly a half-hour for the kid to mix all the paint, but finally he finishes. He loads all the quart cans into a box. I pay and leave.

We drive back to the White House. It is late, after ten by now. Polly is positively giddy. She chatters away and plays with the car radio, switching the dial between FM and AM. Finally, she finds a New Age station she likes and sticks with it. Tangerine Dream is deep into some mellow chords. Polly rolls down her window; it is February and cold, but she doesn't seem to mind. Washington is beautiful at night. The BMW zips by the Washington Monument, the Lincoln Memorial, a half-dozen other national landmarks, all bathed in golden incandescent light. A million headlights stream by us as we drive. They appear to be frozen on the highway, as if they are part of a photograph that was taken in a very long shutter speed so that the cars are blurred but the headlights are frozen. I find it all very sensual. The car is dashing down Pennsylvania Avenue now. We're very close to the White House. Polly unties her blonde hair and lets it flow in the breeze. She laughs and turns the radio up louder.

I approach the White House driveway that leads to the West Wing. I stop at the guard station, which is along the ten-foot-high black iron fence that runs along Pennsylvania Avenue the length of the Executive Mansion. A White House policeman with a dog on a leash approaches the car. The dog sniffs around the car, then he is pulled off to the side of the driveway by the cop. Above us and around us, motion sensors and cameras kick on. I've been working here long enough to know something about White House security. I know a man on the roof probably has a rifle trained on the car at this moment.

At first, the guard won't let us past the gate. He doesn't recognize Polly, although I think he knows the car, which makes him suspicious. Polly is fishing in her purse for her White House parking pass and can't find it. I have a feeling he is very close to ringing his Secret Service bell when Polly finds the pass. This satisfies the guy and he opens the gate. We're in.

Quickly, we park and enter the West Wing. There are night lights on in the Office of Policy and Planning but everyone has left. Apparently, it is even too late now for Rebecca, Luis, Sam and Wayne.

We go to work. Polly and I have picked out a dozen colors. All bright, all incandescent, all radioactive. There will be a main color, though: a deep purple named Wild Napa Grape. Polly will be doing most of the painting, I will just follow along, doing as she says. The four white walls of Polly's office will be our canvas. We will leave the baseboard and the other trim Tuscan Beach, to frame the colors.

She takes off her overcoat and jacket, kicks off her pumps and dips a four-inch brush into a can of Wild Napa Grape. Meanwhile, I cover the furniture with dropcloths and then tape the woodwork.

Polly starts by painting long, wide streaks across the walls, letting the brush take over her hand. I watch in amazement. She slaps the paint on seemingly in random swipes, but soon I see there is method to her work. Each stroke is precisely timed, each line is thought out in advance, each sweep of the brush starts where she wants and ends where she wants. She has changed colors now, but she hasn't bothered changing brushes. She dips her brush deep into a quart of Hollyberry, which is a hot pink. The horizontal strokes soon become vertical strokes, then horizontal again. She is going bolder now with the Hollyberry, but then she suddenly finds a new color—a deep red named Lipstick—and she grows even bolder with it.

I follow suit, slapping on strokes of Ruffled Iris, Vibrant Violet and Grape Vine. Polly counters with Mulberry Bush, Mixed Berries and Radicchio. My old friend Raspberry Sorbet makes a surprise appearance. I decide to step back and go with some mild colors, so I swab on some pastels, such as Pansy Petal, Cloudberry and Drowsy Lavender.

We work feverishly. I'm growing weary as the hour grows late, but I see no sign that Polly intends to slow down. She has a radio in her office and is playing a classical music station. The orchestra plays a Wagner overture, and while the pitch rises and the beat hardens and grows louder, Polly stays right with it, almost stamping her feet as she slaps the walls.

The woman is a true artist.

Painting the White House

I need a rest. I collapse onto a dropcloth and bundle some rags behind my head. I watch Polly work. I glance at my watch. It is past three o'clock in the morning. Most of the room is finished. It is awash in a splash of purples and paisleys. Polly is using one of the half-inch brushes to paint manic portraits of Muskmelon fish on the wall behind her desk. Tiny Foxglove Pink bubbles stream up toward the ceiling, where they break the water. She has painted other little scenes on the walls here and there: birds in flight, planets in orbit, rivers running wild. On the wall directly opposite her desk she has painted an abstract nude in Prussian Plum. It is a stark portrait: the woman's breasts jut out, her legs are opened wide to expose her pubic region, her mouth wide open, her tongue exposed. She wears an expression of defiance. I stare at the nude, and I conclude that Polly has painted a self-portrait. She has exposed herself, and she has no shame.

I am thinking about all this as I fall asleep.

* * *

When I awake, I find Polly in my arms. We are twisted in each other's limbs on the floor of her office. She is asleep. Her head is resting on my chest. We are fully clothed, but I still think we shared something close to a sexual experience.

For a few short hours last night, we shared brushes but we shared much more. We dabbed our brushes in paint, going from can to can, exchanging their colors as though we would exchange our body fluids. We climaxed together while laying down colors on a flat, smooth surface. And then we came down from our high as the latex dried.

The room is our child.

I blink open my eyes.

We are surrounded by empty and half-empty quart cans of paint. The drop cloths are still down. The room, though, is finished. I nudge Polly. She opens her eyes slowly, then looks at me and smiles.

"I think we better clean up," I tell her. She nods and lifts herself off me, then stands up. She stretches and tells me she is stiff. I stand up and ache all over as well. I haven't fallen asleep on the floor since my days going to frat parties at George Washington. I sit down behind her desk and rub my eyes and the back of my neck.

Suddenly, I notice Wayne standing in the doorway.

He says nothing. Polly sees him as well. She is running her fingers through her long blonde hair, trying to stroke out the knots. I glance at my watch. It is just past seven-thirty. Wayne has arrived for work early, I guess.

Wayne takes in everything he sees. I follow his eyes as they inspect the room. The outer office is bathed in Tuscan Beach. Here, we are surrounded by a Wild Napa Grape haze. He sees the fish, the birds, the planets, the river. Finally, his eyes find the nude and he stares for a moment; then glances at Polly, and then glances at the nude again. I think he knows it's her, but I don't think he understands why it's her. Finally, he turns and leaves.

I bury my head in my hands. I have a headache. I need sleep in a soft bed. I am going home and screw off the rest of the day. No way can I paint another room today, not after painting this room last night.

I lift my head. Suddenly, I hear a muffled chime. Polly's phone is on the floor, a few feet from where I am sitting. It begins glowing a light green shade—I would guess something close to Viridescent Velour. And then Ocean Kelp letters appear across the screen of Polly's phone. I can see the message. It is from Wayne. It says:

What the hell is going on in there?

"Polly, look at this."

She strides over and picks up her phone. She shakes her head, then types a response.

It says:

Fuck off, Wayne.

* * *

I am sure that I will be fired because of the paint job in Polly's office, but I never hear a complaint. I find out, though, that Tom had a purple shit fit when he saw the walls and the fish and the birds and the planets and the nude and everything else, but he doesn't bitch to me about it. We stay friendly in the weeks following the night in Polly's office and he occasionally sneaks into a room I am working on and helps me out with a brush or roller for an hour or so.

Certainly, Janey isn't going to fire me. Not after our motorcycle ride.

So my job is secure.

Painting the White House

I hear Polly's office received a new coat of paint. I don't know who painted Polly's walls. Certainly not me. Perhaps Tom and his assistants did the job themselves. That wouldn't surprise me. As I believe I have told you, they are very capable house painters.

As for the color, I'm told her office was not painted in a coat of white, which I would have expected to happen in the Office of Policy and Planning. No, it didn't get another coat of Tuscan Beach, but it did receive a drab pastel color. Well, you can't expect miracles. Change takes years, you know.

Anyway, I really shouldn't be commenting on the matter because I have never actually seen Polly's office since our night of Wild Napa Grape. I sort of heard from Tom's people that I should do my best to stay out of the Office of Policy and Planning.

Polly left the White House shortly after our night of Wild Napa Grape. Still, she occasionally sends me an email. She is living in Soho with a male model named Monroe.

So far, she hasn't sold any paintings but she and Monroe aren't starving. Polly was quite frugal during her three years in the White House and managed to bank virtually all of the $150,000 a year she earned as a chief aide in the Robbins Administration. She writes that she and Monroe have enough to live on for a few years, so at this point she doesn't care how her paintings sell. She is working again, painting pictures again, and that is all she cares about.

Not too long ago, I emailed her back asking if she could send me a small painting, something for my apartment.

A few days later, I received a framed acrylic of a manic Muskmelon fish.

The Kahana Bay Room

Iris and I have a nasty fight over the color for the China Room. The room is, of course, where the First Lady displays the White House china. All the First Ladies starting with Dolley Madison have displayed white or bone china, or some variation thereof. As such, the room has always been painted white. Then, Janey Robbins comes along and orders a pastel blue china for the White House. The stuff sits there for three years and let me tell you it never looks right.

So Iris and I have decided to paint the room blue to match the china. Good idea, but we can't agree on the shade. I argue for something nautical. From the samples, I pick out Freeport, Narragansett, Kahana Bay, Oceanside, Hang Ten, Sea View and City of Annapolis. Iris is having none of it. She argues for something metallic: she suggests Roller Coaster, '57 Chevy, Lone Star State, Motor City or Parachute. We argue for hours. Iris, I can tell, is in a foul mood and I'm not sure why. Our mental and verbal gymnastics have always been practiced with great gusto and no ill will toward one another; I have, indeed, looked forward to our weekly jousts over tint, shade and hue. This time, though, our sortie is tinged with a hint of mean spiritedness; at least it is on her part. Her troubles are weighing heavily on her and I suspect she is using our argument over the China Room as a way to release evil energy. I don't think this has anything to do with the color for the China Room.

Still, she holds her ground and insists on something metallic. Clearly, she is leaning toward '57 Chevy. But I can be a stubborn guy as well, and

Painting the White House

I hold out for a nautical tone for the room. We take the dispute to Hazel, but she won't help this time. I think she knows what is troubling Iris and wants to keep her distance.

The day ends and I go home that night without the issue resolved. This upsets me, because it means I can't stop at a paint store on my way to work the next morning since I don't know what shade to tell them to mix up. My night is restless. I find it difficult to sleep and when I do doze off I don't dream.

The next morning I arrive at the White House ready to pick up the fight where we left off the night before. Oddly, though, Iris tells me to select whatever color I want and not bother her about it.

Iris has relented too easily and I don't understand that at all. It is as if all the fight has gone out of her. I know how tough she can be when she wants and I have never known her to be a quitter when she thinks she is right. All this concerns me, of course, but I have my own job to do and I am already behind schedule. I dash out to a paint store and order up a half-dozen gallons of Kahana Bay. I return and hunker down to work.

The hours go slowly. Call it a painter's sixth sense, but I can tell something is very wrong in the White House. I can tell by the way people don't talk when they walk down the hallway outside the China Room. I can tell by the way the quiet rests uneasily outside on the South Lawn. I can tell by the way the White House parking lot is filled to overflowing. It means everybody with a parking pass has been told to be on duty today because something big is going down.

By mid-morning, I am well into my work in the China Room when Iris comes to see me.

"This is goodbye," she says.

"Goodbye? I don't understand."

Perhaps, I think, I have been fired for painting Polly's office purple, after all. That's my first thought, but I realize by Iris's expression that this has nothing to do with Polly's purple walls.

"I'm leaving," Iris says. "I've been fired. Tom wants me out of the White House. He leaned on Abe and Abe leaned on Janey. This morning, Janey came into my office and told me that I've been dismissed."

"Why? What's this all about?"

"Tom is certain that I leaked the story about Warren to the guy from the *New York Times*. I denied it, but Janey said it was out of her hands.

She said it didn't matter whether she believed me or not, Abe made up his mind and that was that. She said she was sorry, but she had to support her husband on this."

Iris sits down on an early American chair covered with flowered upholstery. It sags under her weight. She sighs.

"I can't really blame them. They need a scapegoat and I happen to be convenient."

Iris passes her palm over the wrinkles in her dress, extending her hard-glossed fingernails. Today, she is wearing a truly awful combination of pink top with orange skirt. On her, it doesn't work. I think the mixture of hot colors in the fabric clash with her cool blue eyes. During my months working in the White House, I often wondered how a woman who could have such a keen eye for color and style could be such a hopeless failure when it comes to picking out her own clothes.

"You aren't going out without a fight, are you? I mean…you can't let Tom get away with this. Janey is her own woman, she can change her mind on something like this. Why don't you go back and talk with her again? I'm sure you can make her believe you didn't leak that story."

Iris shrugs.

"It's too late for that. I'm not the only one who is being fired today. Right now, Warren is in the Oval Office and Abe is firing him, too. I don't blame Abe for that. You can't have a chief of staff trying to kill himself, particularly if he tries to do it in the White House. After Abe fires Warren, he is going to fire Warren's staff. He is going to do a complete housecleaning. There will be a total reorganization of the White House staff. Tom Thatcher will come out of this with enormous power. I don't think he's going to be awarded the title of chief of staff, but he's going to be the guy in charge. When Abe picks a new chief of staff, I'm sure he will be nothing more than a titular officeholder. Tom will be the one in charge."

Iris stares at the floor for several minutes.

"Maybe it's a good time to get out."

Personally, I have mixed feelings on all this. I have grown to like Tom and admire his ability with a paint brush. For someone who had never picked up a roller until a few weeks ago, he has made tremendous strides forward as a house painter. I wouldn't mind having him on the job with me in a time of need. I bet he doesn't mind climbing up a ladder, either.

Painting the White House

Still, I'm not sure he's the right man to be running the White House. Tom may be great in his role of assassin. He may be a terrific hired hit man, an excellent terminator, a wonderfully cold and calculating serial killer, a regular maniac in the tower, but would I want him running the White House?

I ask myself those questions and decide that, no, I wouldn't want him in charge of the most important house in the world.

I think Tom Thatcher lacks the cerebral ability to think things out. Maybe in time, after he's painted a few rooms and rolled on a few more gallons of interior flat latex, his judgment may improve. But now is not his time.

Iris would be a much better chief of staff, I conclude.

"What are you going to do now?" I ask.

"I think I'll go back to Blue Pickum for a few months, spend some time with my Gram. I haven't seen much of her since I came to Washington and I miss her. I'll probably eventually go back to law school, which was always my intention after leaving here, anyway. I don't think I'll enroll back at Georgetown, though. I think I'll look for a school in the South. I'm probably going to end up in civil rights work, anyway, so I might as well go where I'll be needed."

Iris rises to leave, but I jump to my feet first and put my hands out, motioning her to sit down again.

"Do me a favor?" I ask. "Don't go anywhere just yet. Just stay put. OK?"

I don't know what I can say or do, but I think I might be able to save Iris's job. I leave the China Room in search of Janey. I am sure I could appeal to her, that I could change her mind. I also think I can plant the idea in her ear that Iris would be perfect for Warren's job. I'd even give her another motorcycle ride, if that's what it would take.

I search the White House, corridor by corridor, poking my head in room after room after room. I stop people in the hallways and asked them if they know where I can find Janey, but they all beg off, refusing to tell me where the First Lady may be. For an hour, I search fruitlessly. It is a frantic search and one conducted without much thought. I find myself dashing helter-skelter through the corridors, looking in the same rooms two or three times. On the second floor, I crisscross the East Hall, checking the Lincoln Sitting Room and then the Queen's Sitting Room, and then the Lincoln Bedroom and the Queen's Bedroom. I feel as though I am a character in a 1960s drawing room comedy. Red Buttons should be playing me, I decide. This scene should be shot on black-and-white film. It should show Red racing from room to room, opening doors and slamming them closed again. I dash downstairs. Janey isn't in the Red Room, the Blue Room, the Green Room either. There are some tourists in the East Room. They are gathered around the great gilded Steinway piano that serves as the centerpiece for the room. It is a truly magnificent musical instrument. A docent is telling the tourists about it.

"Anybody see the First Lady?" I blurt out.

They give me curious looks. I feel foolish and leave.

Finally, I spot Van Buren and Webster. I ask them whether they know where I can find Janey, and I ask them knowing that they know where she is. It is, after all, their job to know these things.

I also know, deep down, that they will tell me. We have become friends during the past few months. I have heard them speak of the people they are sworn to protect, and I can tell they harbor a certain amount of disdain for them.

You see, there are two types of people in the White House: the people who come and go every four or eight years and the people who stay here all their lives.

The people who leave when the administration changes are, of course, the president, his family and political staff. They are temporary occupants. The American people have agreed to let them hang around so that they can do the very temporary job of governing the country. As Warren Adams told me early on, politics is cyclical and nobody who occupies the White House by virtue of an election should expect to be here more than just on an as-needed basis. To these people, the White House is merely temporary housing.

The other type of people who occupy the White House are permanent people. They are the gardeners, the cooks, the fix-it guys, the housekeepers, the ushers and the Secret Service agents. They are really the people who do run the White House, and all of them know, deep down, that Presidents and First Ladies come and go, but the maintenance staff stays on forever. As such, the permanent White House workers do their best to tolerate the temporary people. It is a constant love-hate relationship and there is never harmony between the two sides. There is always friction in the White House yin and yang. I think that may be a main reason the country always seems to be in a mess.

By virtue of the U.S. Constitution, however, the temporary people have considerably more power than the permanent people. The temporary people know this and the permanent people know it as well.

That causes great hatred between the two sides.

And then along comes me. Am I a permanent White House person or a temporary White House person? It's not a question I can answer. After all, I am here temporarily, really just until I finish painting the White House, and yet although I am a temporary occupant of the Executive Mansion I have no powers to govern. On the other hand, my job as painter is more akin to the jobs held by the permanent people—certainly, I have more in common with the White House carpenter than the White House press secretary.

And so I am neither, but it is clear to me that the permanent people trust me and they are willing to help in my time of need.

"Where is Janey?" I ask Van Buren. "Do you know?"

He nods his head. "She's in the State Dining Room," he says.

Webster gives me a smile. I've always found him a strange sort of fellow, but I think he wants to bond with me now. The smile tells me to watch my ass. Good kinesics on his part.

I blurt out a thanks and trot quickly down the Cross Hall. Seconds later I'm standing at the entrance of the State Dining Room. I haven't spent much time in here because I haven't painted the place yet.

It is a cavernous room that is used for only the most opulent formal affairs. It has thirty-foot-high white walls, a white ceiling with a cornice of white plaster and a huge rococo-revival chandelier dangling overhead. The centerpiece of the State Dining Room is a long rectangular mahogany table surrounded by fifteen yellow Queen Anne chairs.

Kings and queens have dined here, sat on these yellow chairs and debated matters of state with each other and the president. Heads of state have been feted at this table. Ambassadors, congressional leaders, Supreme Court justices, Cabinet officers, great generals and admirals, diplomats, authors, actors, statesmen, billionaires and astronauts have all sat at this table, sharing meals with the President and First Lady.

Right now, I find Janey Robbins sitting in one of the Queen Anne chairs at one end of the table.

I am surprised to find her daughter Jodie sitting at the other end.

* * *

It is the first time I have seen Jodie since she was sprawled across Mrs. Lincoln's bed, wearing the kimono given to her by the emperor of Japan. Today, she is wearing bluejeans and a red Spandex top. Her kinky hair is tied behind her head showing off large gold hoop earrings. She is wearing no make-up, which is fortunate for her because I can tell she has been crying. Her mother has been crying as well.

"Is this a bad time?" I say.

Janey shakes her head. "No...please come in. We were just having one of those mother-daughter things."

Oh-boy-this-is-great, I think. I'm here to plead for Iris's job, to nominate her for chief of staff of the White House, but I have the distinct impression that I have just walked in on the ultimate final confrontation between Jodie and her mother.

"You know my daughter...the college student?" says Janey.

She says it with a generous amount of kinesics, intended to make me understand that Jodie is no college student. Of course, I already know that, but I never saw the sense in telling Janey.

"Did you know she was kicked out of Yale? Not too many people know that. We managed to keep it very quiet. How would it look if the daughter of the president of the United States gets kicked out of Yale?"

Janey looks at me as she says this. I know she is not expecting an answer out of me.

"So we make some calls, talk to people, pull some strings and we find a place for our little scholar here at Dartmouth. Know what happens next? She never shows up for class. Shit! She never even shows up to be interviewed by the admissions committee. Instead, she goes skiing. Skiing! In fucking Vail, Colorado!"

Janey rises from the table and paces through the State Dining Room. She walks with her hands on her hips and circles the table, never taking her eyes off her daughter. Janey is wearing a string of white faux pearls over a blue suit of jacket and skirt. She looks very Barbara Bush, but without the white hair. The pearls jangle back and forth as she walks. She asks me a question that I know is really directed at her daughter.

"How can it be possible that Abraham Robbins, the president of the United States and commander in chief of the armed forces, and his wife, the First Lady of the United States, have no idea that their daughter has just spent the last two months hanging around the slopes and screwing every ski instructor west of the Rockies?"

"How did you find out?" I ask.

Janey turns to her daughter and smirks.

"The credit card bill came yesterday."

Jodie folds her arms across her chest and smirks back.

"We sent Air Force One for her last night. After I finish with her, I intend to speak to her Secret Service agents. And when I finish with them, they are going to be on igloo guard duty in Alaska."

Jodie rolls her eyes up to stare at the ceiling. I know what's coming next.

Any mother who has a daughter in any household in America dreads this day. Just because Janey happens to live in the White House does not exempt her.

This is the day when the daughter finally rebels against the mother, the day when there is no turning back. This is the day when the daughter tells the mother that she sleeps with men, and that she likes it, and that she has been doing it since the age of fourteen. This is the day when the daughter tells the mother that she has hated all the clothes the mother has bought her since the daughter was twelve years old. This is the day when the daughter tells the mother that she is planning to move in with her boyfriend, and that he is not going to medical school, but he does have to keep regular appointments with his probation officer. This is the day when the daughter tells the mother that she drinks beer and smokes grass and has had an abortion because she kept forgetting to take her birth control pills. I'm not sure Jodie is going to admit to all that, but you get the idea.

Anyway, this is the day all that happens, and it just so happens that it is happening today in the White House.

* * *

Janey talks on. She tells me Jodie has had all the advantages. She tells me that she and her husband sent her to the best private schools, that they spared no expense to make sure she had the best prep school education money could buy. Whenever Jodie showed that she was weak in a certain subject, Janey says, she and her husband went the extra mile and hired tutors for her.

"If I had known she was going to turn out to be such a dummy, we could have saved our money," Janey says.

I really want to leave. I stand up slowly, but Janey hisses at me: "Sit down!"

I sit.

"Now, look at her," she continues. "A failure at Yale, a failure at Dartmouth, a success on the ski slopes."

Jodie has sat through all this abuse, saying nothing. Mostly, she inspects her nails. I wonder whether she is still having a split cuticle problem. More likely, she is simply using her body language to show me she is ignoring Janey. Maybe she was paying attention during linguistic anthropology class, after all, and has picked up a technique or two in kinesics.

"I bet we have the first First Daughter to flunk out of school," Janey says. "Margaret Truman, Carolyn Kennedy, Luci Johnson, Julie Nixon, Susan Ford, Amy Carter, Chelsea Clinton, Jenna and Barbara Bush, Sasha and Malia Obama, even Ivanka and Tiffany Trump—all of them are modern, successful, intelligent, bright young women who brought something to the... "

Janey stops speaking. She rolls her eyes and I can tell she is looking for just the right word. Finally, she finds it.

"All of them brought something to the Office of the First Daughter," Janey asserts.

"Janey!" Jodie shouts, at last.

She stands up quickly and strides over to her mother. She arches her back and slaps her palms onto her hips. "The Office of the First Daughter? What the hell are you talking about? I never wanted to be First Daughter, nobody ever asked me. All I know was that I was having a good time in high school when you and Dad came along one day and said, 'Sorry, little girl, but you have to grow up now. Your daddy is going to be president of the United States, and you are no longer allowed to be a teenager, you are no longer allowed to go out on real dates with boys, you are no longer allowed to enjoy the final years of your youth. So please, hurry up and become a responsible adult.'"

She paces back and forth in the State Dining Room. Her face is very flushed. "Come to think of it," she says. "You never told me that Daddy was going to be the president. I think I read it on Snapchat."

Painting the White House

Jodie sits down and shoves a hand into her jeans pocket. Her jeans are tight and she has trouble pushing her fingers into her pocket. Finally, she works them all the way in and withdraws a vaping pod. She lights up. I have a feeling her mother has never seen her vape.

She takes a deep drag and exhales out a gust of blue smoke. She stands up again and waves the hand holding the e-cigarette at her mother. The smoke forms tiny little curlicues that have trouble keeping up with the motion of Jodie's hand.

"Now, after we've been here for three years I suddenly find out I have been elected to the Office of the First Daughter? And not only that, but I am lousy at the job!"

Jodie shakes her head, holding back tears. She collapses in her seat.

"Janey," she says. "Fuck you."

Janey jumps to her feet, clearly enraged. She strides over to her daughter and stands over her.

"Don't use foul language around me young lady," Janey snaps back at her.

"Damn you!" Jodie says.

"Damn you!" Janey counters.

Cripes, I think, what the hell am I doing here? Poor Iris. This is not the time to bring up her troubles. What can I do?

I decide the best strategy is to leave. I will dash back to the China Room and make up some type of story and talk Iris into hanging around the White House for a while longer. My next plan is to approach Tom, to talk him into reconsidering, to appeal to his intellect—to talk to him man to man, painter to painter, to convince him to talk the president out of firing Iris.

"This is a bad time," I tell Jodie and her mother. "I'll come back." I start backing my way out of the room.

"Don't go!" Janey snaps at me. "I want somebody I trust to hear this."

"That's right," says Jodie. "Don't go."

She turns to her mother.

"I trust him too, you know. I trusted him enough once to show him my body."

Jodie points to me with her thumb.

"He has seen me naked," she says, quite defiantly.

Cripes, I think.

Janey is stunned. A thousand thoughts must be running through her mind at this moment.

"Is that true?" she says.

"It was...uhh...it was...uhh...it was..." I sort of wave my hands back and forth. I can't seem to make the words come out. I find myself forced to communicate entirely through kinesics.

"It was completely harmless," says Jodie, coming to my defense. "I was sleeping in one of the bedrooms upstairs when he walked in to paint it. I slept nude that night because I had just slept with one of Daddy's military aides."

Cripes, I think.

"Which one?" shrieks Janey.

Jodie sits back and puts her feet up on one of the Queen Anne chairs. "I don't know," she says. "I don't remember his name. I don't think he told me."

Cripes, I think.

Janey rises from her seat and paces the floor, walking from one end of the mahogany table to the other. "Are there any other little secrets you want to share with me?"

"Give me time," Jodie says. "I'll think of some."

* * *

Actually, it turns out there isn't that much more to tell. Jodie tries to shock her mother with lurid stories of sex and hedonism, but Janey stops listening and starts sobbing.

Somehow, that touches Jodie. She starts sobbing as well, and soon the two women have embraced. Jodie soon apologizes to her mother for all she has done and Janey apologizes to Jodie for neglecting her.

I can't say they really resolve their differences today, but they bond through each other's misery. I wonder whether Janey will tell Jodie about her own pursuit of physical pleasure, and I decide that she probably will not. Above all, Janey is still her mother, and she would lose that edge over her daughter if she admits to many of the same weaknesses that afflict Jodie.

I know, however, that from now on Janey and Jodie will become good friends and they will try to share experiences more often. It may be tough to do in the White House, but I guess it is tough to do in anyone's house.

Painting the White House

Meanwhile, by now I am sure that Jodie and Janey have forgotten that I am in the room. I slip out quietly and jog back to the China Room. Iris is not there. I run up to her office. She isn't there, either. I ask Hazel where she has gone, and Hazel tells me I missed Iris by about ten minutes. She cleaned out her desk and left the White House.

I suddenly realize that Iris never told me where she lives. I can't call her because I don't know her phone number.

I don't know where Blue Pickum is, either.

But I'm sure I can find it on my GPS app. Another motorcycle trip south? Maybe. This time, without Janey.

11
The Vista Mist Bedroom

In protest of Iris's dismissal, I have decided to paint the remaining rooms in the White House white. I'm not sure anyone will notice my act of defiance, but if anyone asks me why I am painting all white from now on, I will tell them it is in protest of the firing of Iris Jefferson. I hope Tom asks, because I intend to tell Tom, painter to painter, what I think of him should I see him.

Anyway, I work late to finish up the China Room. I plan on starting early and working late through the remainder of the job. I'm also going to work on weekends and holidays. I want to be finished painting the White House as quickly as possible. Actually, I'm almost through as it is. All I have remaining is a handful of rooms.

One of them is the Queen's Bedroom. For years, it has been painted in a pastel shade of pink. Visiting royalty usually sleeps there, hence the name. Its most distinguishing feature is a magnificent four-poster bed that was brought into the White House by my old friend from the twenty-dollar bill, Andrew Jackson.

As I said, I plan to paint the room white. I select Vista Mist. Vista Mist is a very white white. I'm really not putting much thought into the selection of colors from here on in. With Iris out of the White House, all my enthusiasm for the job is gone.

I stop at a paint store on the way home from work that night and ask them to make up four gallons of Vista Mist. I plan on starting early and working late again tomorrow. Maybe I can finish the room in one day and move on to the next room, which, as you know, will also be painted a very white white.

I leave the paint store with four gallons of Vista Mist in hand, and decide I am still angry and don't feel like going home. I decide to drive around the city for awhile to cool off. Maybe I'll stop for a drink, maybe I'll stop for something to eat, maybe I'll stop and see a movie. I don't know what to do, so I just drive. Twenty minutes goes by, thirty minutes, forty minutes. I'm really not paying much attention. I find myself on Connecticut Avenue near the entrance to the zoo, which is where I saw the monkeys yawn not too long ago, and I decide that a walk around the zoo might give me a chuckle, might make me feel better, might help clear my head. Hopefully, I'll see the monkeys yawn again and that will make me laugh. But it is late and the zoo is closed. I wheel the truck back onto Connecticut Avenue and drive some more.

I make some right turns, then some left turns and I'm on Massachusetts Avenue near the U.S. Naval Observatory, which is near where Nancy and Franklin live. I wonder if Nancy is home. I wonder if Franklin is home. I drive the few blocks into Georgetown, make my way to N Street and drive by their townhouse. I see the lights on in their apartment. I park a few blocks away and walk toward their home. I pass the Gannt-Williams House, the Decatur House, the Laird-Dunlop House and the Foxall House. I have always loved this neighborhood, loved the Victorian architecture, the red brick walkways, the green ivy on the walls, the urban trees turning yellow in the fall, the whole ambiance of Georgetown. I have never forgiven Nancy for sleeping with Franklin and ruining our marriage. It meant that I had to leave her and leave Georgetown. I'm on their block now. I approach their front door and raise my hand to ring their bell, but I suddenly decide against it. I walk away quickly, hoping the shadows will hide my form. I'm not sure why I want to see Nancy and Franklin tonight; probably I just want company. I find my truck and leave.

I'd like to see Iris and talk to her but I don't know where to find her. I don't know where Polly lives, either, and I'm not even sure she is still living in the city. I am alone in the nation's capital tonight and I don't want to be.

I drive further and realize I am growing weary. Perhaps, I should just head home and to bed. I'm back on the Mall now, heading up Constitution Avenue. I pass Seventeenth Street. The Ellipse is on my left, and beyond that, the White House. It is bathed in incandescent artificial light, standing out impressively against the black background sky.

The Washington Monument is on my right. It, too, is bathed in bright light.

I approach Fifteenth Street. Very quickly, I pass the figure of a man. He is standing on the double yellow line in the center of the street. He is no panhandler. He is dressed well.

It is Warren Adams.

I wrench my truck into a U-turn and park illegally. I jump out of the cab and race to the center of the street. Yes, it is Warren. He is wandering down the double yellow line, oblivious to the traffic that is whizzing by him in both directions.

He seems to be dancing a jig, gently bouncing from one foot to the other on the asphalt between the two yellow lines. I wonder what symphony Warren hears now. I'm afraid only Warren knows.

I take his arm.

"Warren! What are you doing?"

He glances at me and his eyes light up.

"It's you! My favorite painter! Come to save me from my death again!" He laughs.

I have a million questions, but I don't want to talk to him in the middle of Constitution Avenue. Dodging traffic, I shepherd him over to the sidewalk. He sits down on the curb. I join him.

"I'm cold," he says.

He isn't wearing an overcoat. It is a cold night in late February. I'm wearing a jeans jacket with a red-checked flannel lining. It was a gift from Nancy when we were still married. "Take mine," I say, and I start unbuttoning my jacket.

He puts up his hands in protest. "If you give me your coat, then you'll be cold. You keep it."

"Can I take you home? It's late, your family must be worried about you."

He shakes his head and shivers again. I don't know what to say to Warren, how to help him. For reasons I can't explain to myself, I search my pockets looking for something to offer the man—a gift of some sort. It was I who talked to Eddie Carter, and even though I didn't say anything

Painting the White House

of value to him, he wrote his story and that led to Warren's dismissal from the White House staff. I know it isn't my fault, but I feel strangely responsible for this whole mess. I want to make a peace offering to Warren, to give him a present that lets him know I am sorry that he was fired today.

Finally, in my pocket I find a roll of antacids. They have a mint taste. It's dark, so I'm sure he can't see the label.

"Mint?" I ask.

He turns to me and smiles.

"Thanks, but I don't want one."

I shrug and pop one into my mouth. I'm not sure why I did that; I certainly don't have heartburn now.

We are silent for a few minutes. The cars race by. It is late, but not too late. There is still a lot of traffic on the streets, a lot of people still on their way home from work, a lot of Washingtonians on their way out for the night. A lot of people coming and going, a lot of people with a purpose. At this moment, I don't think Warren has a purpose. I'm not sure I do, either.

Suddenly, Warren says, "Did you know I was fired today?"

I did know it, but I decide to feign ignorance. I shake my head.

"Abe Robbins called me into the Oval Office today and told me I had to leave the administration. He said he couldn't have a suicidal chief of staff. He said he was very sorry, but I had to leave. He's planning a press conference tomorrow to announce my resignation. He says he'll dance around the question of suicide, that he won't mention it in his remarks, but he is sure the press will ask about it and if they do he plans to be honest with them."

"How do you feel about that?"

"I guess he has no choice."

He then tells me that he hasn't been to work since the *New York Times* story was published, that he has remained secluded in his home. Several reporters camped outside his house for a few days after the story made the paper, but they eventually gave up and left.

He says he is glad to leave the White House. He says he never liked the job of chief of staff, anyway. He says he is also glad that Abe fired him, because it gives him a chance to go out the way he wants to go out.

"You know, it puts me in pretty select company," he says. "Not too many people have been fired by the president of the United States. I bet all the presidents put together have only fired a few dozen people after all these years."

He thinks about that for a few minutes. I know how much importance Warren Adams places on his role in history. In a way, he may finally have found his niche in the history books.

"What did you say when the president fired you?"

"I said, 'Fuck you, Abe.'"

He laughs at that.

"I bet I'm one of the only people in the entire history of the republic who has had the balls to say 'Fuck you' to the president. What do you think of that!"

I tell him I don't know what to think of it.

He continues.

"Want to know something else? I didn't just say, 'Fuck you, Mr. President.' I said, 'FUCK YOU, MR. PRESIDENT. FUCK YOU AND FUCK THAT WHORE OF A WIFE YOU HAVE, AND FUCK THAT SLUT OF A DAUGHTER, TOO!' I shouted it in his face as he sat across his desk from me in the Oval Office. I spit those words out with great delight and great gusto, and then I repeated them so that there would be no mistaking it. 'Fuck you, Mr. President,' I said, 'Fuck you.'"

He rubs his hands together to warm them. I can see his breath form clouds in the chilly night air as he exhales. He blows on his hands.

Warren turns to me. "I really did tell him off; I'm not making that up. How many people tell off their boss? Just think of all the millions of Americans who would love to have traded places with me today—not because I told off the president, but because I told off the boss."

By now, I am convinced that Warren Adams is nuts and he should have been fired. I do, however, have a certain amount of empathy for him. If he is nuts, it is life in the White House that has made him nuts.

There is probably more to it than that. He is convinced that he has always been the better man than Abe Robbins, that he deserved to be president more than Abe. But party politics, the whims of the electorate and the cyclical nature of realpolitik conspired against Warren to deny him his due. I'm sure that has festered in him for years and helped drive him over the edge.

He has already tried to kill himself once and had it not been for me he would likely have succeeded. Having been denied the one opportunity he gave himself to commit suicide, Warren did the next best thing. He told off the president, and when he did it he made sure there would be no going back. Now, it is likely that he won't be invited to the next national convention, he won't be offered a chance to make a speech, he won't be asked to attend a fund-raiser for the president. He will no longer be a Washington insider. Having failed to kill himself in the physical sense, Warren succeeded in killing himself politically.

I think he took a great deal of satisfaction from that.

"I told him exactly what I thought of him," Warren says. "I told him that I was a better congressman, I told him that I wrote more important legislation than he did, I told him my list of achievements was far superior to his. I told him he never could have won the election without me and that he will never win the next one now that I'm gone. I told him all that, and I would say it all over to him again."

Warren leans back on his elbows and lets his head drop back so that he is looking at the sky. It is a clear, moonless night. The late winter air is still above us. I lean back and look skyward as well.

He speaks again.

"Do you know I'm very good with constellations? It is sometimes hard to recognize them when you look at the sky in the city because of all the street lights, but if you look closely and let your eyes adapt, you can see patterns in the sky."

I gaze at the sky. All I see are dim stars.

"There, to the left. . .that's Orion, the hunter. See that star in the corner of the constellation? That's Betelgeuse. The other bright star in the constellation is Rigel. The fuzzy patch in the middle of the constellation is the Orion Nebula."

I look, but I don't see.

"Do you know there is a solarium on the roof of the White House? It is really quite a romantic place and it has a tiny balcony that looks out over the entire property. Luci and Linda Johnson used to bring their boyfriends up there. Amy Carter used it a lot, too, although she was much too young for boys when she lived in the White House. But Amy had a telescope and she set it up on the balcony and studied the stars with it. Imagine that! Amy Carter knew about constellations."

He points out other constellations as well. He shows me Taurus, Ursa

Major, Leo and Gemini. He tells me the two brightest stars in Gemini are Castor and Pollux, and he shows me where to find them in the sky. He shows me Camelopardalis, Cassiopeia, Cepheus, Monoceros, Pyxis and Puppis. He knows all their names and that impresses me. He shows me all the stars and constellations and he talks a great deal about planets and galaxies and star clusters and nebula. He says I could see all that just by looking up in the sky at night. I gaze skyward, and wonder why I have been missing this wonderful show all these years.

"Do you know," he says, "a lot of people think stars are just white, that they have no color? That isn't true. Stars are blue and red and they have other colors as well. They give off light in the infrared and the ultra-violet spectrums. Some stars are even black. Sometimes, it is tough to tell what color a star may be. Look up at the sun and it may appear to be yellow, but often when the sun sits on the horizon it is red. From space, I'm sure the sun appears to be white. But how do you explain sunspots? They seem to be black, but they are actually very very white. The joke is they just aren't quite as white as the rest of the sun, so in contrast they appear as though they are black."

That's a lot to think about. I want to tell him to slow down so that I may ask some questions, but he keeps right on talking about stars and their colors.

"Astronomers study stars by the spectrum of colors they emit. They can even tell whether stars are moving toward us or away from us by their color. It's called the Doppler Effect. Stars just aren't little dots of white light, you know, they are very colorful."

I squint at the night sky. I start to see patterns made by the stars, but if you ask me to point them out to you, I would probably have a lot of trouble doing it. I don't see any colors in the stars, though. I guess that takes practice.

Still, I stare skyward. I decide that the White House needs somebody who can recognize the constellations, somebody who can look skyward and see something other than dim dots of white light, somebody who can see color in the stars, somebody who has vision.

Warren Adams has vision. Tom Thatcher doesn't. Iris Jefferson has vision. Janey Robbins doesn't. Polly Morris has vision. Wayne Marks does not. I never asked Polly and Iris about constellations, but I'm sure if I did they would be able to name dozens of them, and they would be able to point to the sky and show me the patterns made by the stars. And I bet they would know that some stars have color and some stars do not.

Those are the type of people we need in the White House and I wish they were still there. But no, Warren, Iris and Polly are out. Tom, Janey and Wayne are in. That should tell you something about the White House and all of fucking Washington, for that matter.

Maybe there is a way to get Warren Adams back to the White House. OK, I agree with the president. You shouldn't have a chief of staff trying to kill himself at the same time you're trying to run the country. But the government is filled with advisors, aides, consultants and other people who have no real jobs, they are just kept around to offer an idea or two when they are needed.

I think Warren should be kept around the White House to be the government's chief sky watcher. That's right. I think that whenever President Robbins has a knotty problem on his hands, he should call Warren in for consultation. The appointment would be at night, of course, because that's when the constellations are out. Abe would order all the lights in the White House turned off, particularly all the lights that light up the outside grounds at night, and then Warren and the president would go out on the South Lawn and stare at the sky.

Warren could point out star patterns to the president and that would help clear his mind. I think if the president looked at each constellation as a puzzle and each star as a clue to solve that puzzle, he would be able to see the solutions come together. After all, when you look at the sky as a whole, you see the problem as a whole and you see all the stars laid out in the field, and after awhile you see how they form the constellations and how easy it is to solve the problem.

I lean back again and gaze at the dome of the sky above me. The constellation of Orion is now familiar to me and I also recognize Gemini. The two bright stars in Gemini are Castor and Pollux, and I see those stars as well and recognize them.

I turn away from the sky to tell my idea about White House stargazing to Warren, but he isn't sitting next to me anymore. I look around quickly—behind me, to the left, to the right, but I don't see him. While I have been sitting on the curb gazing at the constellations overhead and thinking about their colors, Warren Adams has walked away.

I call his name out a few times. Certainly, he can't have walked too far.

I stand up and look around some more, and then I spot him.

He is back in the middle of Constitution Avenue, walking along the double yellow line. He is walking away from me.

"Warren!" I shout.

He turns around and waves. It is a short wave, really nothing more than a flip of the hand to acknowledge me. I think I also catch the hint of a smile. Then, just as a Greyhound tour bus comes motoring through the intersection, traveling about forty-five or fifty miles an hour, Warren Adams steps away from the double yellow line.

And in front of the bus.

"Noooooooooooo!" I scream, and as I scream I find myself running toward him.

Everything becomes a bluish blur to me. I can hear myself scream, I can hear the bus's air horn, the screech of its tires, the impact of human tissue on foreign-made steel. I see the colors of the human body explode in front of me, and then I scream again.

The bus driver doesn't see Warren until it's too late. The tour bus, which had left Ohio that morning with fifty Jaycees aboard, strikes Warren's wiry little body and propels him forward about thirty feet. Then, the bus runs over him. The bus' right front and right rear tires roll directly over Warren Adams, crushing him under the weight of the huge vehicle. I see it all.

I hear some horns blaring around me and realize that I am in the middle of Constitution Avenue as well. I dodge my way back to the curb. I find myself crying. I can't compose myself. I drop to my knees and sob like a baby. I hear sirens. I see flashing lights. I don't know how long it takes, but the police have arrived. One of the DC cops sees me weeping and comes over. He asks if I have seen the accident. I tell him I haven't. He tells me I should leave the scene. I do.

I find my truck and drive home. It is difficult going to bed but somehow I manage to find sleep. It is welcome; I do not try to fight off the sleep that my mind and body need. The next morning, I rise early, eat a quick breakfast and head right for the White House. I work hard on the Queen's Bedroom that day, and I work hard on the next room I paint and the next room I paint after that.

Now, I have one room left to paint.

Lord, how I want to finish this job.

12
The Atomic Winter Office

Sunday morning. It should be my last day in the White House. I am eager to finish.

I've been up since six. I want to start early because there is no telling how long I'll be able to work today. Before she lost her job, Iris told me to save this room for last and paint it on a Sunday. Even then, she said, there is no guarantee I would be able to work uninterrupted.

So I arrive at the White House just a little before seven. I quickly unload the truck. I have brought five gallons of Atomic Winter with me this morning. Atomic Winter is aptly named. It is white, of course. As you know, I have pledged to finish up the White House with white paint. But how best can I describe the white of Atomic Winter? Sort of like the surface of the moon, I think. Not the white of a bride's wedding dress, not the white of a lotus petal, not the white of a dandelion puff, not the white of one of Warren's stars. Those are the whites of life. Atomic winter is barren, desolate Death Valley white.

White without life.

Perfect for the Oval Office, don't you think?

I laugh at the thought as I make my way through the West Wing and approach the door to the Oval Office. It is slightly ajar. I see a light on as I near the room. Already, I know I have been thwarted today.

I am sure that President Abraham Robbins is at his desk at seven o'clock on a Sunday morning. It means I can do no painting today. Iris did warn me about this.

Still, I continue to walk toward the Oval Office. There is a magnetic attraction that pulls me forward; I am unable to resist. For three months I have been working in the single most unique building on Earth—and yet, isn't this just a rectangular structure of bricks and mortar not unlike any other house in America? What makes the White House so different from, say, the house at 1602 Pennsylvania Avenue?

Every room I've painted inside the White House is simply just a room. True, some of these rooms are quite elaborate; they are furnished with expensive antiques and priceless works of art, but when you come down to it, they are simply ordinary rooms—nothing more than enclosed interior spaces with doors and windows. They are no different than any room in your house or mine. They are places where people sleep at night, eat meals during the day, talk out their problems, laugh, cry, fornicate, carry on with their lives.

There is no difference between the Red Room or the Blue Room and the room at the zoo where the monkeys yawn. A Louis XVIII chair in the Yellow Oval Room is—when you come down to the basics—just a piece of wood that you can use to plant your ass. It offers the same function as the red vinyl bean-bag chair in Nancy's apartment and is probably a lot less durable.

But still, I'm not sure that description applies to the Oval Office. This room is different—it is a singularly unique room that contains furniture unlike any other furniture in the world. In the Oval Office, you do more than just sit on the furniture. In this room, you plant your butt in a chair and you talk over problems that affect the entire world, the entire future of the human race. No other room on the planet can harness that power.

From the Oval Office, FDR beat Hitler and Tojo and Woodrow Wilson kicked the Kaiser's ass. Hoover screwed the country and Nixon screwed himself. And does anyone know whom Kennedy may have been screwing?

Johnson quit the presidency here and Ford and Carter fucked up the presidency in this room. Reagan goofed off. And Harry Truman unleased the atom bomb on the world.

And right now I find myself approaching its threshold.

* * *

Everything inside me, every cell within my brain, every sinew in every muscle in my body, every volt of electric current pulsating through my neurons and synapses, tries to make me stop walking this walk. Still, I go forward. I should turn around, return to my truck and go home. Tomorrow, I should talk with Janey or Tom or somebody like that, and ask them when I can paint the Oval Office. They will tell me when the president is next scheduled to be out of the country or, at least, out of Washington, and I will wait until then to paint his office. It may be tomorrow or the next day, it may be next week or next month. I may have to wait quite a long time before I can paint Abe Robbins' office. That is what I should do, but still I walk forward.

I stop in the doorway and gently glide the door all the way open. It is true, the president is at his desk. I see him, but he has not noticed me as yet. I am quiet and make no noise. I still have time to turn back, to go home, but I remain in the doorway. How long am I in the doorway? A few seconds? A few minutes? A few hours? I don't know, I have lost my sense of time.

The Oval Office reminds me suddenly of Checkerboardland.

I scan the room. It is the largest office I have seen while I have been working in the White House. Certainly, it is bigger than Polly's office. I estimate that it is about forty feet from front to back, thirty feet from side to side. On the floor is a Prussian blue carpet. At its center is an embroidered eagle—a mirror image of the bas relief eagle that dominates the white plaster ceiling above.

The furniture is early American. The wood is dark mahogany with black wrought-iron hardware. The upholstery on the chairs and sofas are earthen colors—mostly oranges and ochers. I find it all very masculine.

The desk is huge and Abe Robbins seems lost sitting behind it. I guess that it was probably designed for a much bigger man.

Behind the desk are great French windows, perhaps twelve feet high. They bathe the room in stark yellow sunlight. It almost hurts my eyes to look directly at the windows. On either side of the window are flags. One is the American flag, the other is the blue flag with the presidential seal.

There is a lot of marble in the room—pedestals for small sculptures, a small table by the door, a mantel over the fireplace. Carved into the mantel are these words:

I pray Heaven to bestow the best of blessings on this house, and on all that shall hereafter inhabit it. May none but honest and wise men ever rule under this roof.

Above the mantel is a painting of George Washington.

He isn't smiling, either.

Finally, I remember why I am here. I am, of course, here to paint the Oval Office. I am here to finish the job I began four months ago. I am here to bring an end to my professional relationship with the President, the First Lady, the others.

"Pardon me?" I say.

Pardon me?

Well, what would you have said?

Abe Robbins looks up. He is reclining in his chair, his feet up on his desk. He is wearing a blue flannel lumberjack's shirt, tan sports slacks, white sweat socks, white tennis shoes. He is tan and trim, his hair a lively salt and pepper. He wears glasses to read. *The Washington Post* Sunday edition is open on his desk. Clutched in his hands are the color comics, which he had been reading when I entered the doorway.

"Yes?" he says.

The president has a deep voice. He enunciates well, which I guess is a talent he picked up while spending most of his adult life delivering speeches. I can tell all this from the way he said the word "Yes." I believe the president is such a forceful speaker that he may have no reason to rely on kinesics.

"I'm here to paint the room," I tell him.

He looks genuinely surprised.

"Christ! Was that supposed to be today? Why doesn't anybody tell me about these things? I'll get out of your way in a few minutes, I was just looking over some things."

He returns to his reading. He doesn't smile while he reads the comics. Where is it written that once you become president you lose your sense of humor?

I decide to start work, so I put down the cans of Atomic Winter and then go back into the outer office where I have left my dropcloths, my rags, my brushes and rollers and everything else I'll need for the job today.

Painting the White House

I return to the Oval Office. I find the president has put down the comics and is now deep into reading a thick sheath of documents. I try to make more noise than necessary in the hope that he will become frustrated and leave. I clank some cans together and when I mix up the first gallon of Atomic Winter, I make sure that I bash the stirring stick against the side of the can as many times as possible. I hope he picks up the message.

He stares at me and appears perturbed.

"Hey, painter!" the president shouts. "Knock it the hell off or I'll have your ass kicked out of here!"

Well, I didn't expect him to say that. I feel very foolish, a bit embarrassed.

"Sorry, Mr. President," I say.

He frowns, then goes back to his reading. I go back to work as well.

I have most of my dropcloths down and am well into taping the baseboard when I realize he has been watching me. I steal a glance now and then and conclude that, yes, it is true, he is definitely watching me.

I wonder whether I should turn to face the president and ask if he needs anything. Maybe I should ignore him. Maybe I should just leave and come back another time.

"I'm watching you because I was just remembering my days when I helped out my Uncle Morrie on the weekends," he says with no prompting from me. "Uncle Morrie was a house painter. When I was in high school I worked for him on weekends, and he paid me a dollar an hour. A dollar an hour! Pretty cheap son of a bitch, eh?"

I shrug my shoulders and say, "When I went to work for my first painting crew, I made three dollars an hour and was damn happy to get that."

He laughs.

"I like house painters. I was one myself. They are working people, unlike most of the slobs around here. They know how to work with their hands and they know how to use their heads. I always listen to what house painters have to say."

Suddenly, I decide that I like the president more than I did a few minutes ago. I am sorry that I selected Atomic Winter for the Oval Office. I think this president deserves much better, something with color.

* * *

He lays down the papers he has been holding in his hands.

"Tell me," he says, "why did Warren kill himself? I know you were with him the first time he tried it, and I know you were with him out on Constitution Avenue when he tried it the second time and succeeded. So you can tell me, what was his problem?"

His tone of voice tells me I can speak frankly.

"His problem was that he knew he was good enough to be president, but he knew it was politically impossible for him to be president. That's what he told me. I guess he wanted to be president more than he wanted anything else and couldn't have it. I guess something snapped inside of him."

The president leans back in his chair, cradling the back of his head in his hands. His feet are still on his desk. I can see a smile cross his lips.

"Oh, I guess there's some truth in that. Yes, Warren was never going to be president, but politics didn't have anything to do with that. If Warren thought politics was going to be his problem, then Warren was just not a very good politician. You can always beat politics. Warren's problem was he didn't have the balls to be president. You've got to be a real bastard to want this job and keep it, and Warren was never a very good bastard.

"He didn't understand power. He understood government and he understood those assholes in Congress, but he didn't understand the meaning of power. I liked Warren and trusted him and he was a good friend, but I probably would have fired him after the next election. He was weighing us down here. Every time we ran into a roadblock in Congress or in the courts or the Middle East or anywhere, Warren always wanted to talk it out, negotiate, give a little, take a little."

Abe screws up his face when he says that. He furrows his brow. I can tell he is putting an emphasis behind his disdain for negotiators. I make a mental note to remember each one of his facial expressions because I am sure this will make a wonderful chapter for Nancy's book. She may be able to devote an entire chapter to presidential kinesics.

The president continues.

"Now, a guy like Tom Thatcher—he understands power. He understands it and relishes it; he wallows in it like a pig wallows in mud. He feeds off power and grows fat with it. Tom doesn't know much about government and he doesn't know anything about Capitol Hill—and I don't even think he knows that much about politics—but he knows a lot about power.

"He knows, for example, that when you walk into a restaurant and the waiter sits you at a table you don't like, you don't have to stand for that. Tom would tell the waiter to find him another table and if the waiter gave Tom a hard time, Tom would bitch very loud and he would let everyone in the restaurant know that he works for the goddamned president and you know what? He would get his table. A guy like Warren. . .shit. He would sit at the lousy table and stew in his own soup."

He finally takes his feet off the desk.

"Do you know whose desk this is?" he asks.

I tell him I don't.

"It originally belonged to Rutherford B. Hayes. Did you know that? I just had my feet up on President Hayes' desk. What do you think of that?"

I say nothing.

"There's only one guy in the world who is allowed to put his feet up on Rutherford B. Hayes' desk, and that's me. I have the power to do that. If Warren had this job, he'd never put his feet up on this desk. He'd be afraid he'd get the top of the desk dirty. See my point?"

I nod.

"When I first became president, the General Services Administration asked me whose desk I wanted. It wasn't exactly a question I had expected, so I did some reading up on the presidents and their desks. I read that Queen Victoria gave this desk to President Hayes: it was fashioned out of timbers from a ship that had sunk up near the Arctic Circle. Later, Franklin Roosevelt used this desk and so did Jack Kennedy. So I told them I wanted President Hayes' desk, and a couple of days later two guys from General Services show up with the desk. They drive their truck right up to the guard station out on Pennsylvania Avenue and they start unloading it."

The president smiles as he's telling me this story.

"'Wait a second,' the guard says to the two jerks. 'What the hell are you doing? I don't want the damn desk, take it up to the White House.'

"These guys tell the guard that they work for the General Services Administration and their responsibility is to deliver the desk to the White House, but they aren't allowed to go further than the main gate. The National Park Service runs the White House grounds, they tell him, so if he wants the desk to make it into the building, he's got to call the Park

Service and have them send a couple of guys around to carry the desk indoors.

"The guard is smart. He orders them not to move, then he calls the White House switchboard and tells the operator what's going on."

"What did the operator do?" I ask.

Abe points to himself with his thumb. I can tell he's really proud of what he's about to tell me.

"She calls me. She tells me what's going on. Man. . .I got my ass down to that gate in two minutes. I even walked out of a Cabinet meeting. I told those two jerks to pick up the goddamned desk and get it in here or I'd have their asses. You should have seen the look on their faces! I bet both of those idiots crapped right in their pants! Imagine the president of the United States of America coming out of the White House and telling you to move your ass!"

I am picturing the scene as he tells me the story. Wish I could have been there to see it.

"You know, I never really understood power myself until I walked into the White House. Over in Congress, I had political power. I could move legislation. I was pretty good at it. . .regardless of what that asshole Warren may have told you. I was a good congressman, a good senator. I took care of my constituents and never lost an election.

"But I never had what you would call real power, because no matter what I did, I always had to convince several hundred people to go along with me. I was always just one vote, when it came down to it. To me, it was very frustrating—to wield so much influence on Capitol Hill, but to have no real power.

"I thought about getting out of politics many times over the years, but I never did. Know why? I knew that as long as I was in Congress and as long as I kept doing good work, I would always have a shot at becoming president. If I had quit, I could have gotten a job at any hot-shit law firm in the country. . .and I didn't even need to do that. My father-in-law owns a bunch of supermarkets and I could always go to work for him. When he dies, I'm going to get the supermarkets anyway. I'll have millions of dollars when that happens.

"But no matter how rich you are, you don't have real power. Sure, you can own a string of supermarkets and be responsible for thousands of employees, but what does it matter? They don't need you. . .they can always find jobs somewhere else. You may have millions of dollars, but your power is only as limited as your money. Even billionaires don't have unlimited power. Get my meaning?"

I wasn't sure I did, but he wanted to talk and I wanted to listen.

"When I first thought about becoming president. . .I mean, when I first sat down and seriously considered it, I asked myself why I wanted the job. I made up a list. I wrote down a lot of bullshit, like I wanted to make people's lives better, I wanted to be able to disarm nuclear warheads, I wanted to feed the hungry, clothe the needy, shelter the homeless. . .that sort of thing. I worked on that list well into the night until I could barely keep my eyes open. And then, finally, when I was finished I looked at the list and had myself one hell of a good laugh. I took out a fresh pencil and crossed out every word I wrote on that list, and then at the bottom of the page I wrote one word. Know what that word was?"

I knew.

"Power."

He jumps to his feet and comes striding out from behind Rutherford B. Hayes' desk.

"Right!" he says.

He turns back toward the desk and starts shuffling around, looking through some papers. After a few minutes he finds what he is searching for and turns back to face me. It is a thick sheaf of papers clipped together.

"Let me tell you about power," he says, as he holds up the sheaf. "Know what this is? It's an application for a federal grant written by some loopy college professor. She wants ten million dollars to study something called kinesics, whatever the hell that is. I don't know what she's talking about, although I read somewhere in here that it has something to do with monkeys and yawning."

He rifles through the sheaf, then tears out a page. "This is a letter written to me by one of the people who works for Tom Thatcher—his name is Louie or Lewis or some name like that. Anyway, Tom's guy says in the letter that he has reviewed the grant application and determined that the professor's project has significant scientific and cultural value. He says the American people will benefit if we give this college professor ten million dollars to study why monkeys yawn.

"Now, I want you to understand something. I have a lot of confidence in Tom Thatcher and the people who work for him. They have never given me bad advice. I don't know anything about what this college professor wants to study and frankly, I couldn't care less whether she watches the monkeys yawn or she watches the monkeys fuck. The money is no big deal, either. Hell, we have lots of money around here. I could easily find ten million or even twenty million for Ms. Science here. And so, since Tom's people have endorsed this grant, then I, as president, would be foolish if I didn't follow their advice. Right?"

"Right," I agree.

He laughs, and then he drops the report in the trash can next to his desk.

"I'm president and I can do whatever the hell I want," he says. "I can do that because I'm a powerful son-of-a-bitch."

* * *

President Robbins leans back to stretch. He tells me he rose early and came down to the Oval Office before breakfast. He says he comes to the office a lot before breakfast. It is a quiet time, even on weekdays, because the staff hasn't arrived for work yet and he can catch up on his reading.

I'm thinking about Iris. What the hell, I figure, I may as well make a pitch for her to be chief of staff.

"Why did Iris have to lose her job?" I ask.

"Tom told me she leaked the story about Warren's attempted suicide to the *New York Times*," he says. "I can't have that here. If your people aren't loyal to you, if they do things like leak stories to the press, then you have to get rid of them."

"But Iris says she didn't leak the story. . .she denied it all the way. Why didn't you believe her?"

He turns quickly to face me.

"Whether or not I believed her never mattered," he snaps. "Get it? It didn't matter to me whether she was lying or telling the truth. That's all there is to it. OK?"

He says "OK" but his body language tells me it's not OK.

"OK," I say.

He wears a very sour look. He rubs his chin. I think he has something more to say on the issue, but he hasn't decided whether to say it. Finally, he speaks.

"I knew Iris wasn't the leak."

Huh? What?

I'm about to say something to express my astonishment, but I don't have to use verbal communication. He can tell by the look on my face how astonished I am by this sudden revelation.

And then he surprises the pants off me again.

"Franklin was the leak."

"Are you sure?"

He shoots a stern glance at me—his kinesics are truly excellent—telling me that the president of the United States certainly is sure and I, a lowly house painter, should know better than to ask.

"But if Franklin was the leak, why did Iris have to. . ."

He raises a hand to silence me.

"That's enough," he says. "OK?"

"OK," I say.

He pauses, and I think he's sorry that he was short with me. Still, I'm thinking that he will not listen to my arguments about saving Iris's job.

I decide it's best to make small talk, so I ask him how his wife and daughter are doing.

"Jodie is a good kid, but she's weak," he says. "We never should have sent her off to Yale; she wasn't ready to leave home. I blame myself a lot for what has gone wrong with her. I should have been a better parent, but when you're president you have to neglect your family. That's a fact.

"I think I can make it up to her now, though. We'll keep Jodie around the White House for awhile. We'll make her a hostess or an usher or whatever the hell we can find her to do. We'll give her some responsibility and see how she responds. Maybe, in the fall, we'll try another college—maybe American or George Washington—a school she can attend during the day and then come home at night.

"Mostly, I think she needs to stay away from her mother. And I think Janey needs some time away from the White House. This place can make you crazy and I think Janey needs a break from it all."

He tells me this while he is looking out the windows behind his desk, staring at the Rose Garden. Since it is early March, nothing is yet in bloom. Still, the landscaping is magnificent.

The president turns to face me, then cocks an eyebrow.

"I hear the First Lady likes to go on motorcycle rides. Can you believe that?"

Cripes, I think.

I tell him I find that hard to believe. He gives me a smirk, then turns to face the Rose Garden again. I think he knows.

"Anyway, I'm planning to send Janey off to Europe for a few months. She'll like that."

He turns to me and smiles, then sits in the chair behind the desk and puts his feet back up.

"Everything should come together very nicely. By the fall, Jodie should be back in college and she'll have all this booze and sex and dope out of her system. She'll study hard and she'll be the model of the perfect American college student. By late fall her mother will come home from Europe. She'll have spent months hobnobbing with the royalty and getting her picture in the European newspapers. I think she'll have forgotten all about motorcycles by then. She'll be rested, fresh and ready for what's ahead."

"Ahead?" I ask. "What's ahead?"

"My next campaign, of course. Late in fall, I'll announce that I'm running for another term. I'll need my wife and daughter to campaign for me, particularly in the early primary states like Iowa and New Hampshire. You know, if I had to run tomorrow I don't think I could win, what with a wife who likes to go to white trash bars on the back of a motorcycle and a daughter who likes to drink beer and have sex in the Lincoln Bedroom with junior military aides. Do you think the American people want to see that type of behavior from their president's family?"

I shake my head.

"The best thing we can do is move them out of the way for a few months. There's a lot to do around this place and the last thing I need is my family being a pain in the ass and causing me grief."

He takes his feet off his desk, sits forward and starts sifting through his paperwork. He spends a few minutes looking for some documents; when he finds them he holds them up to show me.

"Right now, I have to find somebody to replace Warren. These are FBI reports—background checks on about a dozen people who are under consideration for chief of staff. I guess I'll have to pick somebody, but it won't be an easy choice."

I'm about to suggest Iris's name, but he cuts me off.

"It's going to be hell around here for the next few months. The new chief of staff is going to get into a pissing contest with Tom right from the beginning. Tom got rid of Warren and now he thinks he has the real power in the White House. The new guy will have the title of chief of staff and he's bound to think that means something around here, so I expect him to give it right back to Tom with both barrels. It's going to be quite a showdown."

I have decided not to suggest Iris's name to the president for the job of chief of staff. Iris is a fighter. She's tough and I think she can handle the likes of Tom, but I don't want to put her through it. I like her too much to see her in Warren's job.

I tell him, "You sound as though you are looking forward to this and that you would pay money to watch the fight."

His eyes brighten. "You're damn right! I sure would pay money to watch this. And not only that, but I'm going to do my best to make sure it's a knife fight to the death. I want to see plenty of blood and no rules. I'm going to watch this whole thing from the sidelines, as though I'm watching the Cleveland Browns and the Green Bay Packers stomp the living shit out of each other."

"But why?" I ask. "Why run your White House that way?"

He smirks at me.

"You haven't been listening. The White House is all about power, and if you're going to work here you better know something about power. You asked me why Iris Jefferson had to lose her job. I'll tell you why: because I said so. I don't care whether she was the leak or Franklin was the leak. But I do know this: I'm the president and I decided she had to go and now she's gone. That's power and that's the way it works around here. You want to know why there isn't money in the federal budget to study why monkeys yawn? Because I say there isn't, and that's power and that's the way it works around here.

"Tom knows about power. He out-wrestled Warren and now he thinks he's the heavyweight champ. Fine, let him think that. But now, I'm going to throw a new guy into the ring. Maybe Tom will lose this one, maybe he'll win again. I don't know, but it sure will be fun to watch."

He thinks that over for a few seconds.

"And then you know what?"

I shake my head.

"When one of them thinks he has this thing won, when one guy thinks he has beaten the other guy, I'll step in and shake my big fat ass at both of them—just to give them the message about who has the real power around here."

He laughs at that. I don't.

"Come on, why look so surprised?" he asks. "Presidents have been acting like bastards for hundreds of years. Do you think I'm the first son-of-a-bitch to ever work in this office?

"Take Nixon, for example. Now, there was a guy who knew what power was all about. He understood it, but he also abused it and he really spoiled it for the rest of us.

"Before Nixon got into office, the president could be powerful anywhere he went. He could almost be regal. Guys like Franklin Roosevelt, Harry Truman, Jack Kennedy, Lyndon Johnson—they could go anywhere in the world, bark an order and people would jump through hoops.

"Kennedy and Roosevelt were terrific at that—they always knew how to use power. They were born with it, and when they became president they knew what to do with it. But then Nixon came along and abused his power and now things are different. Sure, the president is still a pretty powerful guy, but when he leaves the White House grounds he has to watch what he says and does. Every word, every gesture, every action has to be measured. The only place where you don't have to do that, the only place where you don't have to give a shit what you say or do, is right here...inside the White House."

He pauses on that thought, then rises and faces the Rose Garden again. He clasps his hands behind his back. And then Abe Robbins says, somewhat wistfully, "In here, I'm king. Out there, I'm just the president."

* * *

I've heard enough. I have the feeling that Abe Robbins thrives on the power of the presidency. That saddens me. I have decided he is not a very good president, and I tell him so.

"How can you play with people's lives this way? You manipulate everybody: your daughter has troubles, so you bury her in the White House until she sobers up. Your wife has troubles, so you pack her off to Europe and hope she burns out. Your chief of staff kills himself because he can't measure up to your ideals, and now you are preparing to offer up a new victim to the wolves around here. I think you're a terrible human being,

Painting the White House

and I am disturbed and embarrassed that you're my president."

Let me tell you, it isn't easy telling off the man who has just proclaimed himself the most powerful human being on Planet Earth. Warren was able to tell off his boss, but Abe drove him to it. Besides, Warren was crazy and I'm sure he knew during his last meeting with Abe that he was going to kill himself and, therefore, Warren didn't care what would happen. Maybe he wasn't so crazy, after all.

Me? I'm not crazy, I'm just an ordinary house painter.

When I finish my little speech, I look at President Robbins and can tell he is genuinely hurt by my remarks. I guess he doesn't hear a lot of sass in the White House. I have the feeling that, besides Warren, I am the first person to ever stand up to him in this room. Anyway, I don't think he knows what to say to me, so he just stands there and mulls things over for a moment.

"Did you vote for me?" he asks, at last.

"Yes," I tell him, "I did vote for you."

He looks pained.

"I'm really not a bad person, you know. Everything I do, I do for a purpose. I think I've done a good job running the country. The economy is doing well, people are working, we're not at war."

"What if I had told you that I didn't vote for you?"

He smiles.

"I would have told you to go fuck yourself."

* * *

I think the president has grown weary of our conversation. He gathers up some papers and shoves them under his arm and then he pulls out the sports page of the *Post* and folds that under his arm as well.

"You really do want to start work in here," he says. "I'll get out of your way now."

He starts walking toward the door.

I stop him.

"Before you go, tell me this: What did you think of the color I picked out for this room?"

He looks toward the open gallons of Atomic Winter sitting in a corner of the office. Then, he frowns.

"Looks OK to me."

I know something about kinesics, so I know he is lying.

"And the rest of the White House? How does that look?"

He shrugs. "I'm no judge of these things."

"You mean you don't like the colors?"

"Oh, I guess the colors are fine. . .that's not the problem."

He walks over and puts his arm around my shoulders. He leads me to the window behind President Hayes' desk, and together we look out over the Rose Garden and, beyond that, the South Lawn. The sunshine is bright this morning, brighter than I can remember it in weeks. Soon, it will be spring in Washington—cherry blossom time. I'm looking forward to that.

"Keep a secret?" the president asks.

I nod my head.

"I'm color blind."

"What?"

"It's true. I've been color blind since I was a kid. I can't tell red from blue, blue from green, green from orange, orange from pink. You could paint these walls whorehouse red and I wouldn't know the difference."

I am stunned, completely astounded by what the president has just told me.

He turns to me and smiles.

"I see everything in black and white. That isn't a bad way to look at things, don't you think?"

I nod my head. He has a point.

Epilogue

After the Atomic Winter

Nancy Dewey finished her book on kinesics. It had modest sales. Writing in the *Massachusetts Journal of Linguistics*, Dr. Chandra Srikakulam said Nancy's book "breaks new ground in the fundamental study of non-verbal communication." Her husband, Franklin, was fired shortly after Warren Adams' suicide. He is unemployed, as of this writing.

Polly Morris has had little success selling her art in New York. Her boyfriend, Monroe, works part time as an artist's model. They live on her savings.

Tom Thatcher quit the White House shortly after the next election. He returned to Florida, where he re-established his law practice. He has stayed out of politics. Shortly after arriving in St. Petersburg he bought a beach house and put a lot of money into refurbishing it in the Art Deco style. He did all the painting himself, however.

Sam Finn, Rebecca James, Luis Calaveras and Wayne Marks quit the White House staff when Tom left. All found lucrative jobs in private life. Luis ran for a seat on Los Angeles City Council, but lost.

Van Buren remained in the Secret Service until retirement. Webster eventually quit the Secret Service and wrote a tell-all gossipy book about his years as a Secret Service agent in the White House. He wasn't initially able to sell the manuscript to a publisher. Instead, he self-published, uploading the manuscript to Amazon. For his back cover biography, he used a photograph of himself displaying a particularly off-center application of his toupee. Despite these shortfalls, the book sold a half-million copies and was eventually picked up by a major New York publisher.

Steve, Phil and Jan, who were the Secret Service agents assigned to protect Jodie Robbins at Yale, were transferred to their agency's office in Black Falls, Idaho.

Tad, Ted and Tammy each received credits as research assistants in Nancy's book on kinesics. Later, Tad earned his degree in art history and Ted received his degree in Spanish literature. Tammy learned Greek and graduated with a degree in international relations. Today, Tad works in a shoe store, Ted sells life insurance and Tammy is a cocktail waitress in an Atlantic City casino.

Lieutenant John Anderson, who left his empty scotch bottle behind in the Lincoln Bedroom, was transferred from the White House staff to the U.S. Marines base in Guantanamo Bay, Cuba. He left the Marines at the end of his tour of duty and took a job selling mutual funds. No one has ever believed his story about having had sex with the First Daughter.

New York Times correspondent Edward M. Carter eventually left journalism to write a book about his exploits covering the White House. The book suffered poor sales. When Carter proposed another book, his publisher turned him down. Carter had to take a job as a public affairs officer for the American Red Meat Institute. As plant-based meat substitutes started flooding the fast-food market, he proved himself fully incapable of generating positive publicity for traditional red meat and was eventually fired.

Zachary Green, a White House electrician, was dispatched to the Blue Room to repair the wiring in the overhead chandelier. He never returned from the job. His disappearance remains a mystery to this day.

Iris Jefferson finished law school and opened a practice in Blue Pickum. She is the only black attorney in Blue Pickum and does a good business. Most of her work stems from landlord-tenant disputes. Iris usually represents the tenants.

Jodie Robbins worked in the White House as an assistant usher, then finished college at American University. She majored in fine art. After graduation, her father found her a job in the American embassy in Tokyo, which she had requested.

Abe Robbins won re-election. After completing his second term, he retired to the Main Line outside of Philadelphia to write his memoirs. Abe and Janey enjoy taking long motorcycle rides in the country.

I'm still painting.

Hal Marcovitz spent more than thirty years as a newspaper reporter and columnist. He is also the author of more than 200 nonfiction books for young readers. His other novel is *My Life With Wings*. In 2021, Hal served as co-author of *Notes on Bucks County*, an analysis of the political evolution of Pennsylvania's most unique county. He makes his home in suburban Philadelphia.

If Painting the White House sparked your smile...

 Hal Marcovitz's funny yet thought-provoking *My Life With Wings* is about a newspaper copy editor, Eggerton, who wakes up one day and discovers that he has wings. What is he going to do with them? Eggerton does not seem to easily relish this unexpected development. Instead, he deeply ponders on what his action should be and how will he cope with this new chapter of his life...

 Hal Marcovitz's writing style is also oddly vibrant...This novel is a fine allegory about life, aspiration, and how one perseveres against challenges. Absorbing the fun creative spirit of Marcovitz through this novella will keep readers fascinated from the beginning to the end. Simply put, this is a unique tale and a creditable triumph for the author who has created a book worthy of sitting on a shelf next to the works of other great writers.

 Lit Amri for Readersfavorite.com

www.ingramcontent.com/pod-product-compliance
Lightning Source LLC
LaVergne TN
LVHW010328070526
838199LV00065B/5689